HOTEL TRANSYLVANIA 2

MOVIE NOVELIZATION

Adapted by Stacia Deutsch

Simon Spotlight
New York London Toronto Sydney New Delhi

SIMON SPOTLIGHT
An imprint of Simon & Schuster Children's Publishing Division
1230 Avenue of the Americas, New York, New York 10020
This Simon Spotlight paperback edition August 2015
TM & © 2015 Sony Pictures Animation Inc. All Rights Reserved. All rights reserved, including the right of reproduction in whole or in part in any form.
SIMON SPOTLIGHT and colophon are registered trademarks of Simon & Schuster, Inc.
For information about special discounts for bulk purchases, please contact Simon & Schuster Special Sales at 1-866-506-1949 or business@simonandschuster.com.
Manufactured in the United States of America 0715 OFF
10 9 8 7 6 5 4 3 2 1
ISBN 978-1-4814-4819-2
ISBN 978-1-4814-4820-8 (eBook)

CHAPTER ONE

All fathers get emotional on their daughters' wedding days. But on his daughter Mavis's wedding day, Dracula was taking it particularly hard. When it was time for the ceremony, his three monster friends found him hiding in a closet.

His buddy Frankenstein spoke to the closed closet door.

"Drac, you gotta come out. It's almost time."

The door opened. Dracula came out. He looked awful. His tuxedo was misbuttoned and his shoes were on his hands. He was a wreck.

"Okay! Here I am! Stop yelling at me!" Dracula yelled.

His friend Griffin looked him over. "Pull yourself together, buddy!"

Frankenstein tried to calm him down. "Drac, everything's going to be fine."

"I know that! It's all good!" Dracula answered.

Griffin looked up.

"Then what are you doing up there?"

All three monsters looked upward. Dracula was on the ceiling curled in the fetal position.

"I can't go through with it," Dracula told them. "I won't make it. She's marrying a human! What if it's all a trick, and he's going to hurt her?"

"Drac, you know Johnny's a great guy," Frankenstein said soothingly.

"Yeah, and humans love us now," Griffin added. "I don't want to brag, but my workout video's a best seller."

"I don't care!" Dracula shouted. "I'm losing my Mavy! What if he and his filthy backpack take her away from me for good?"

"Drac, the important thing is, right now you gotta be strong for your little girl. She's gotta be scared too," Frankenstein said.

That did it. Dracula couldn't let his beloved Mavy be scared, even for an instant. He floated down from the ceiling.

"Okay. I'll try. For Mavis," Dracula said.

Mavis was busy getting ready in her room. Her monster bridesmaids were helping her get ready when they heard weird wailing sounds in the hallway.

"What's that messed-up noise?" one of the brides-maids asked.

Dracula entered the room. His eyes were red and watery and his cheeks were streaked with tears.

"Dad! Are you okay?" Mavis asked.

Dracula tried to stay strong.

"Of course I am, Mavy. How about you?"

Mavis looked at her bridesmaids. They nodded and all left the room. Mavis looked at her father, worried.

"Daddy, I love him so much, but am I doing the right thing? He's my zing, but I'm so young! I'm still just a hundred teenager!"

"Girls mature faster," Dracula told her. "And you're practically a hundred and twenty."

"But I didn't realize there's so many things I can do out there! I could be a nuclear pharmacist! Or a mental hydentist! Or I could help people, like a social twerker."

"I never heard of that last one, but it sounds very helpful," Dracula said.

"But, Daddy, if I'm married, am I going to be able to do all that?" Mavis said.

"You'll do it together," Dracula told her.

Mavis took a deep breath. "Thanks, Dad. Why do you look so sad?"

Dracula turned into a bat, and his bottom lip started to quiver.

"It's just . . . the hotel will feel so empty when you and Johnny find your new home. And I'll be all alone."

Mavis was surprised. "What? This *is* my home. I love it here and so does Johnny. We want to build a family here just like you did."

Dracula immediately turned back into his human form. "You're staying? Hooray!"

Mavis smiled. "And . . . you're okay with him not being a monster?"

Dracula shrugged.

"Human. Monster. Unicorn. As long as you're happy."

"I really am!" Mavis told him.

"Then so am I, my little poisonberry," Dracula told her. Then they walked out, arm in arm.

At the wedding ceremony Dracula couldn't hide his emotions. He had written a song especially for Mavis.

> *Where's my little Mavy Girl?*
> *Whose poop I'd wipe away*
> *Protecting her from humans so with Daddy*
>   *she could stay*
> *Good thing that I'm dead, because you take*
>   *my breath away*
> *Seems like only yesterday that you were*
>   *Daddy's girl*
> *Daddy's girl*
> *I'm your batty daddy, and you're my world*

Daddy's girl
His little waif
Daddy's going to keep you, and he'll keep you
  safe because you're Daddy's girl
Daddy's girl
You're my Daddy's girl . . .
Because you're Daddy's girl . . .
Because you're Daddy's girl . . ."

The wedding was beautiful.

Johnny stood at the altar with his backpack. The backpack was wearing a bowtie and held the ring for Johnny to give to his true love.

Johnny's clean-cut brother was a groomsman. Kent, tall and athletic, stood next to an odd-looking monster. He clearly felt a little confused and a whole lot out of place.

Mavis's bridesmaids stood on her side of the altar. Clarabelle, a monster with frog limbs, was next to Johnny's red-haired sister. The shrunken head that lived on Mavis's bedroom doorknob was there too, strung to a coat hanger. She had no body, so her matching bridesmaid dress hung on a small coatrack nearby.

Johnny's other brother Brett was walking down the aisle with Mavis's monster friend Kelsey. Kelsey rolled her eyes and muttered, "I can't believe I'm paired with this loser."

A little red-haired girl (another relative of Johnny's) was a flower girl. She carried a teddy bear and a bouquet of flowers. Everyone said "Awww" as she walked down the aisle. But then a slew of wolf pups noticed the teddy bear and rushed in to pounce on it, shredding the teddy bear and flowers. The little girl was a disheveled mess as the ruined petals fell all around her.

The humans were shocked at the violence, but the monsters thought it was cute. Together they said, "Awww."

It was time for the bride to appear. Slowly, dramatically, Mavis stepped up to the end of the aisle. All eyes, monster and human, were filled with happy tears as they turned to face her.

Dracula held back his own tears as she started down the aisle. Inside, he suffered. His little girl was getting married . . . to a human. He hid his feelings through the ceremony.

Until the end.

When it was time for bride and groom to kiss, Dracula could no longer keep his terror inside. Using telepathy, he threw the shrunken head between them just as Johnny was about to kiss Mavis.

Grossed out, Johnny opened his eyes. Dracula felt a little bad about ruining the moment, but not too bad. He gave in, saying, "Okay, one quick one." They kissed fast before he could throw any other monsters at them.

After the wedding a prickly monster hugged Johnny's dad, Mike. It hurt.

At the reception Marty, the palest monster in the castle, gave a heartfelt, poetic, and completely unintelligible speech. The monsters applauded, but Johnny's family didn't get it at all. Johnny raised his glass, saying, "True. So true, buddy."

The cake screeched in horror as it was cut. The cut slice shrieked like a child separated from its mother. The monsters applauded wildly. Johnny's family grinned uncomfortably while Mavis and Johnny fed each other tiny pieces of screaming cake.

To end the magical evening, Dracula took out his ukulele and very, very, very slowly sang the ending of the song he'd written for Mavis and Johnny.

"Daughter—my one wish for you
As on wings of love you soar
Only love and happiness, now and evermore
Now that you're Johnny's girl
Johnny's girl
Shining your moonlight on the whole wide
* world*
Johnny's girl
And kind of Daddy's, too
Your mommy'd be so happy
'Cause she always knew love is making room
* for all the best in you."*

Mavis ran from Johnny over to her father. She hugged him hard, letting her emotions show and her tears fall. Other monsters started crying too, including Bigfoot. His giant tear fell on Johnny's mother, Linda, soaking her entire body.

CHAPTER TWO

A few years later Dracula was in his room, painting. It looked like a wild impressionist portrait, but it was actually an accurate picturelike representation of the monster posing for him.

Mavis walked in to the room, saying, "Hey, Dad."

Johnny was with her.

"Oh, hey, guys," Dracula greeted his daughter and her husband. He told the monster model, "Gloremus, take a break." The naked model grabbed a towel and went to get some water. "So what's up?"

Johnny said, "Mavis was wondering if maybe you wanted to go for a fly?"

"Oh? We haven't done that in forever. Any special reason?" Dracula gave a strong look at Johnny, trying to determine what the boy was up to.

Johnny responded with a giggle. "No special reason at all. Heh-huh-huh. Right, Mavy?"

He was acting very weird.

"What's his deal?" Dracula asked Mavis.

"He's silly," she replied with a giggle of her own. "It's just a beautiful night and, well, if you don't want to—"

Dracula swung his cape around himself. "No, no, are you kidding? I would eat a bucket of garlic to fly with you."

A moment later he and Mavis stood on the window ledge. Mavis jumped off first and turned into a bat. Dracula followed her down with a fancy dive before transforming. It was a beautiful night for a fly-around, and the two vampire bats were really enjoying themselves.

Dracula pointed out the sights. "Oh, honey, look at those thick clouds!" The sky was heavy, like it might rain. "Remember what we played when you were little? Hide-and-go-seek-sharp-objects?"

He turned to see if she remembered, but Mavis was

gone. Dracula smiled. She was already playing a game. "Oh-ho, okay, regular hide-and-go-seek." The search began. "Where are you? Honeybat! Mavy! I'm gonna get you!"

Mavis peeked out from one cloud, then moved to another hiding spot. Dracula heard her heavy breathing. It wasn't hard to find her. In fact, it was way too easy.

"Honey, are you okay? I couldn't tell if it was you or Frank after he has to put his socks on." He was concerned that she was so sluggish.

"Yes, it's just a little harder to catch my breath since I'm pregnant." She put a hand on her belly.

"Yes, well, I guess that would make it more . . ." He was slow to understand. "What?"

Mavis, the bat, stuck out her stomach to show her dad a little baby bump.

"WWWWOOOOOOOOOHHHHHH-HOOOOOOO!!!!!!!!" Dracula shrieked, his voice echoing in the night. "I'M GONNA BE A GRAMPA!"

He began flying in acrobatic circles, pumping the air with a victory fist.

Down below, in the castle, Johnny was also celebrating. "AND I'M GONNA BE A DAD!"

That night, Johnny sang a song to Mavis's pregnant belly.

> "*'Cause yer Daddy's girl . . . or boy*
> *Daddy's girl . . . or boy.*"

Mavis interrupted. "I'm hungry again, honey. Can you get me some ice cream with anchovies?"

As she said it, her father swooped into the room. "No, no, no," Dracula said. "You mustn't give in to your cravings! It's not good for the baby!" He showed Mavis a thick book called *What to Expect When You're Expecting a Vampire*. He opened to the middle and began to read: "You need to increase your spider intake, so he'll be able to climb ceilings properly. And eat lots of sheep bile."

As he gave the details, zombie waiters delivered dishes made with spiders and sheep bile.

Mavis said, "I love you, Dad, but we don't even know if the kid's gonna be a vampire! I'd be thrilled if the baby's humany just like Johnny!"

That was a shock to Dracula. "Humany? With thousands of years of Dracula genes? Not gonna happen! Here! Just have some monster ball soup. It's your mommy's recipe."

A zombie waiter presented a tray of soup with balls of monster faces gurgling in it.

It was hard to stay firm about the baby being human when the scent of the soup filled the room. Mavis smiled. She loved monster ball soup. "Aww . . . thank you, Dad. Just like you made it when I was a kid. . . . My favorite."

When she started tearing up, the monster balls got choked up as well. One of them gobbled the spoon absentmindedly as they all cried.

Another day went by. Then another week. Another month. Dracula ticked off the days on a baby vampire calendar.

An *X* marked the day when the baby was finally due to be born. That night a monster doctor stopped Dracula, keeping him from seeing Mavis.

"Sir, only the father is allowed in the delivery room," the doctor said.

Dracula didn't like that. "Really? I mean, okay. He's the family, I guess!" He left without an argument.

A short while later, when the baby was born, an odd-looking nurse took it from the monster doctor. The nurse had a deep voice and sounded a lot like he was from Transylvania. It was Dracula in disguise.

He looked at the baby and thought about his wife, Mavis's mother. It was a tender moment for him. Dracula held the baby up facing the graveyard and exclaimed, "Oh, look! It's a boy! It's a boy! Martha! We got the big family we always wanted!" Then he whispered to the baby, "No one will ever harm you as long as I'm here, my little devil dog."

Mavis saw right through Dracula's disguise. "Dad, can I hold my baby?"

"If I were Dad, I'd say yes, but I'm the nurse, Francine." Dracula tried to save his cover. He passed Mavis the baby. "Here you go anyways." He rushed away.

Out in the hallway a zombie orderly, thinking Dracula was a pretty nurse, tried to kiss him!

Dracula roared, flashing red laser eyes.

The zombie orderly backed away. "Myyyy . . . baaaad . . ."

CHAPTER THREE

On Dennis's first birthday he looked like his dad. His red goofy hair stuck up at all angles. At the party he was hanging out at the kids' table with the baby wolf pups. Johnny's parents had come to the castle for a visit. Grampa Mike and Grandma Linda were sitting with the monsters. Frank and his wife, Eunice, were sitting next to Wolf-Man Wayne and his wife, Wanda. Griffin, the Invisible Man, and the Mummy, Murray, were at the end of the long table. Everyone had brought gifts.

"Can't believe Dennis is a year old already!" Johnny said, looking lovingly at his kid.

Grampa Mike agreed. "Is this a handsome kid or

what? Look at that thick, curly red hair!"

Dracula wrinkled his nose. "I don't think it's going to stay red."

"I think it is," Mike countered.

"I think I see some black roots," Dracula said hopefully.

Johnny glanced at Dracula, then gave a troubled look to Mavis.

"I don't think I do," Mike said, staring down into Dennis's hair.

"I have vampire vision. I can see it," Dracula insisted.

Mavis called everyone together. "Okay! Time for presents, guys!"

Murray was excited about the gifts. "All right, let's do this boy up! Check out what I got him—bling!" Murray held up a giant solid-gold medallion on a chain.

"Wow, is it cursed?" Wayne asked.

"Super cursed! Only the best," Murray bragged. "Straight from the crypt!"

Dracula put Dennis on the ground, and the boy stood there for a moment, a bit wobbly as he found his balance.

Johnny lunged forward, saying, "Uh, he's just starting to walk, so maybe it's heavier than—"

Undeterred, Murray put the golden necklace around Dennis's neck. Dennis swayed slightly, took a half step, and then crashed forward, dragged down by the weight of the medallion.

Mavis picked him up. Murray frowned.

"Oh, you're okay, Denisovich," Dracula cooed.

Grampa Mike protested. "His name is Dennis . . . named after my father."

Dracula grinned. "It's not his vampire name." And in a baby voice, added, "My little Denisovichy Weesovichy."

"A vampire?" Grampa Mike looked surprised. "He's got my dad's red hair."

"I don't think it's going to stay red," Dracula said in a singsongy voice.

"I think it is," said Grampa Mike.

Dracula continued in the singsongy voice. "I think I see some black roots."

"I don't see any," Grampa Mike huffed.

"I have vampire vision," Dracula sang out.

Grandma Linda cut in. "Are we sure he's a vampire? Not that it's a bad thing. But shouldn't he have fangs and that pasty skin you guys have?"

Wayne answered, "Technically, you have until you're five to get your vampire fangs."

"Oh, he'll get his fangs. He's a Dracula." Dracula was as certain as he'd ever been in his entire life, which was a very long life.

"He's also half Loughran," Mike said. "Maybe he'd probably be better off where we live. There are more humans there."

The very thought of Mavis and Johnny leaving the castle made Dracula shiver.

Grampa Mike gave Dennis a small toy soldier for a gift.

They couldn't take Dennis away! "What?" Dracula said to Mike. "Look how well he's playing with the wolf pups."

In the corner the wolf pups were giggling with Dennis. One was licking the necklace. Dennis checked out the way the pups played and started licking his new action figure.

Mike grimaced. "Nice influence there." He sighed

loudly, then asked his son, "Honestly, Johnny, you're a grown-up now. Don't you need to get a job?"

Johnny was shocked! "A job . . . ?"

Dracula jumped in to the conversation. "Ehh . . . that's why they have to stay here, because Johnny already has a job."

Johnny tipped his head, totally baffled. "I do? I mean, I do. I mean—what do I mean?"

"Yes, Johnny's in charge of, uh . . ." Dracula stalled until it came to him. ". . . making the hotel more human-friendly. Yes. Here. Staying here. Not leaving." Done and final.

Dracula gave Dennis his gift. The My First Guillotine drew Dennis's interest away from the toy soldier.

Back to competitive grandparenting, Mike and Dracula took turns trying to get Dennis interested in their toy. Mike also tried desperately to keep Dennis from licking the action figure.

While the grandparents battled for Dennis's affection, Johnny considered the job offer. "Yeah, it could be awesome," he said, more to himself than to anyone in the room. "Humans and monsters, sharing the same towels and spoons. That's a huge step for man and monsterkind!"

Grandma Linda was doubtful about the idea. "That's adorable," she said sarcastically. "When Johnny was younger, he had his iguana share a cage with his parakeet. Hope this ends better!"

But Johnny was into it. "Gonna rock it for you, Drac! Don't stop believin'!"

Dennis grabbed the figure Grampa Mike had given him. Mike was thrilled that Dennis chose his toy over the guillotine, right until Dennis giggled and chopped off the figure's head.

Mavis took the guillotine away. "Okay! We just have to baby-proof that."

Dennis grew and grew, and months later he looked even more like his dad than before. His red hair was insane and curly.

"Johnny! Come quick!" Mavis called to her husband. Jonny rushed in. Dracula was with him.

"What's up? He's okay?" Dracula was worried.

"Dennis said his first word!" Mavis cheered.

"He did?!" Dracula got in close so he could hear the word.

"Come on, honey . . . say it again," Mavis encouraged him.

"Bleh, bleh-bleh!" Dennis said in a perfect imitation of Dracula.

"I don't say 'bleh, bleh-bleh'!" Dracula grunted.

"We didn't say you did!" Mavis told him.

"Then where did he get that?" Dracula asked.

"Bleh, bleh-bleh!" Dennis repeated.

"Well, maybe sometimes you say it . . ." Mavis raised a shoulder and gave a small smile.

"I only say it when I say I don't say it!" Dracula insisted.

"Bleh, bleh-bleh!" Dennis said again. And again. And again.

"Okay, kid, we get it. You can talk." Dracula frowned at his grandson, but then, immediately softened. "Denisovich!" He sneaked a peek in the boy's mouth. No fangs. Not yet.

"Dad . . ." Mavis caught him.

"Just checking for cavities," Dracula said quickly, then left the room.

When he was gone, Mavis playfully turned to Dennis and imitated her dad. "Mavy Wavey!"

Dennis giggled. "Ma-ey Wa-ey!"

Dracula zipped back in. He'd caught Mavis telling Dennis what to say. "It *was* you!"

CHAPTER FOUR

For the first time in Dracula's life, the hotel was open to humans. Monsters and humans mingled in the lobby, all dressed for vacation. The lobby had been redecorated with a stand-up video display highlighting the available activities.

The Human Fly, a zombie clerk, and the Grotesque Monster all worked the front desk. They ignored the ringing phone and were crowded around a photo booth app on the Grotesque Monster's smartphone, taking selfies.

When the monster's face was edited into an even more grotesque distortion, the Human Fly exclaimed,

"Oh my goodness, Leonard! If you really looked that hideous, I don't think I could hang out with you!"

They were all laughing as Dracula entered.

"Guys! What's the deal? Is this a party? Pick up a phone!"

The Human Fly hustled to answer it.

The zombie complained to Dracula. "Grrrnnnhhh!"

"I don't care if Johnny said it's a 'cool app'! Johnny's still new here." He turned to the zombie bellman. "Now, Porridge Head, did you call a hearse for the Gremlinbergs?"

Porridge Head was working on a desktop computer. Dracula looked over the zombie's shoulder at the screen. "No! You're checking your Facebook page! Again!" Every answer to every question on the screen was "Brains."

"Drac, I told the guys social media's the best way to promote the hotel. Right, Clifton?" Johnny said as he and the AV-nerd zombie entered.

"Mnnnrrrgghhhh . . . ," Clifton moaned.

"So, Drac, I wanted to go through some thoughts I had as your new human relations coordinating co-assistant, if that's okay," Johnny said.

"Sure." Dracula was half listening. He muttered to himself, "It's a real job. Not a cheap excuse to guarantee Mavis and Denisovich never leave here."

"Right . . . so I was thinking," Johnny went on, "since we have so many humans now, maybe, uh, update some of the acts? Like, maybe the magician?" Johnny thought the shows were stale.

"What's wrong with Harry Three-Eye?" Dracula asked.

"He might be a little old-school for the humans," Johnny said, reflecting on the last time Harry Three-Eye performed his magic act at the hotel.

Humans and Monsters were watching Harry Three-Eye, a three-eyed magician with wings and tentacles, perform his act. His rotten teeth poked out of his head. Harry was wearing a tux jacket and bow tie and sporting a small goatee. His assistant was another ugly monster with a platinum wig. A monster volunteer stood onstage with them.

Harry asked the volunteer, "Tell me, sir, what was your card?"

"The three of spades," the monster replied.

Harry Three-Eye reached into the monster volunteer's body cavity and pulled out the three of spades. "Is this your card, my friend?"

The monster guests in the lounge applauded politely, but humans were grossed out. Harry smugly accepted the sparse applause.

Back to reality, Johnny shook his head. He really hoped Dracula would consider a change.

"No. Harry's great. Can't blame Harry for the crowd not being hip," Dracula said, rejecting the idea of getting another lounge act.

"Okay . . . what about Wayne?" Johnny changed the subject.

"Wayne? Are you nuts? He's my boy!"

Obviously, Dracula wasn't going to change anything in the magic show, so . . . "Maybe something other than tennis?" Johnny suggested. He had another flashback.

Wayne was wearing tight-fitting white tennis pants over his wolf-legs, instructing a human guest. "Okay, so what you want to do is lift the racket right on impact, so you get that nice topspin. Try to hit one." His instructions sounded reasonable.

The human guest bounced the ball and hit it with his racket. That was when Wayne instinctively started to bark, then wildly chased the ball across the court. The lesson ended when Wayne caught the ball and immediately dug a hole in the clay court to bury it.

Johnny and Dracula both snapped out of the memory when the phone rang.

"What is that? What's the noise?" Dracula asked, looking around. He realized the ringing was close. Too close. "It's on me!" he screamed, and started swatting at himself.

"It's just the cell phone I got you," Johnny explained. "Clifton's sending you a text, so you can practice how to write back."

Dracula tried to find the right button to answer, but with his long fingernails it was very difficult. "Ehh . . . gehhh . . . it's not doing it!"

Johnny took the phone. "I got it." He opened the message and read: "'Dear Drac— Ggnnnnggrrrggh.' Now you can text Clifton." He handed the phone back to Dracula.

"All right, fine!" He was willing to try, but his long

vampire fingernails made it impossible. "Gah! How do you do this?"

"It's easy. Look, I'll text Mavis." Johnny took the phone again. He talked as he clicked the keys. "'Psyched for date night.' See? And now look." He showed the phone to Dracula. "She texted right back. 'Gotta cancel. Can't leave Dennis.'" Johnny sighed. "'Ok,'" he texted quickly. "'Are we . . . never allowed . . . to be alone again? I need . . . to feel . . . loved too.'" With that, Johnny finished sadly, "And . . . send!"

"O-kay. All that taught me is that you're pathetic." Dracula was done learning. Texting wasn't for him.

"Yeah," Johnny agreed. "Got it. Maybe you should just get Bluetooth."

That sounded good! "Okay. Bluetooth, come over here!" Dracula called out. A giant blue tooth hopped over with a *boing-boing* sound.

"So, now what?" Dracula asked Johnny.

Time passed and Dennis was now four years old. Grandpa Dracula snuck into his room to wake him up.

"Rise and shine, my Denisovich!" He tousled the boy's red curly hair. It seemed to grow brighter and frizzier with each passing year.

"Hi, Papa." Dennis popped up in bed.

"Hello, my little devil! Did you have sweet nightmares?" Dracula asked.

"Uh-huh . . . I dreamed that I saw a stegosaurus." Dennis was very excited about the dinosaur.

"Oh, and were you drinking his blood?" Dracula was hopeful.

"No." Dennis made an "ick" face.

Dracula sighed. "Just throwing it out there." Dennis began sharing his dream, while Dracula peeked into his mouth. He took out a fang ruler, measured the tooth growth, and then marked the progress in a notebook.

"And he said that, he said that he had a spiked tail because he lived in tropical climates . . . and because he lived in, in the Jurassic period," Dennis mumbled with a mouthful of his grandpa's fingers.

Dracula continued to take measurements and make notes. "Uh-huh . . . Uh-huh . . . You don't say . . . Long time ago . . . yes . . ." Dennis finished, and so did

Dracula. "What a great story. Hey, you want to do something fun?"

Dennis jumped up. "Yeah!"

"I'm going to teach you how to turn into a bat. Like me. See?" Dracula turned into a bat.

"Cool!" Dennis swung out of bed.

"Yes! Cool, like I said! Now, you try!" He moved back to give the kid room.

Dennis pretended to fly, flapping his arms wildly. "I'm a bat!"

"Uh, I mean a real bat," Dracula said.

"I'm a bat!" Dennis announced again, flapping his arms even more wildly and zooming around the room. He made fangs by sticking his teeth over his lower lip. "Fneeee!"

Dracula hadn't thought this through well enough. "Denisovich . . . take a breath. You can really turn into a bat. Start with an arm," he suggested.

"What?" Dennis stopped flapping.

"Just focus, my little Beelzebuddy! Try! Feel the bat!" Dracula tried.

Dennis started flying around again, this time waving

just one arm. He used his head to get speed, bobbing it up and down as he pretended to soar.

"Not a chicken," Dracula told him.

Dennis did a little arm wave and pop-and-lock routine instead.

"For real? We're not doing the electric boogaloo here. I mean, what's going on with you?" He didn't mean to sound so rough, but his tough voice made Dennis's lip quiver. That wasn't what Dracula wanted. "No, no, no, don't be upset."

Dennis started to tear up.

"Please stop crying! Here. Look at me!" Dracula put Dennis back on the bed.

Like a vampire comedian, Dracula flew into the wall, crashing. Dennis kept crying. "Look! I'm flying into the wall!" He continued the act, but it didn't make Dennis laugh.

Dracula crashed over and over until it hurt. That was when Dennis laughed!

"Ahh, yes! It's funny!" Dracula said as he smacked into the wall one more time.

Dennis laughed so hard he fell over. He smacked the

floor and started crying, louder than before. Dracula panicked. He wanted the boy to stop. To get him to laugh again, he stuck his own head in a vice and started tightening.

Dracula's pain made Dennis laugh.

Mavis burst into the room. "Dad! What are you doing? Why did you wake him up?"

"Eh, nothing." Dracula tried to act innocent. "He was having a nightmare so I came to cheer him up. He should be up anyways, it's after eight!" He threw off the vice.

"Dad, don't you remember the new sleep schedule? He's going to human classes half the day." Mavis pointed to the calendar tacked to the wall. "If he could just sleep till two a.m. tonight, it'd be so great for him."

"But, honeydeath . . ." Dracula wrinkled his nose. "Six of Wayne's wolf pups are having a birthday party tonight! You wouldn't want him to miss that!"

"Dad, I love the wolf pups, but they're a little too rough. Dennis isn't safe playing with them at this age," Mavis said.

"Not safe?" That was news to Dracula.

Dennis picked up a Rubik's cube baby-proofed at the corners and started playing with it in his bed.

"Dad, really. Haven't you noticed?" She tipped her head toward her son. "Dennis is . . . different."

"What are you saying?" Dracula asked. "Denisovich shouldn't be around monsters?"

Dennis overheard and chimed in, "I love monsters! Video!"

Dracula grinned. "Ha! See that? He loves monsters!"

"Oh!" Mavis asked Dennis, "You want to show Papa Drac your monster video?"

"Monster video! Let's see!" Dracula was excited. This was a good sign.

"Yay video!"

Mavis put a DVD into their TV.

The announcer on the show asked the kids, "Who's the coolest monster?"

Dennis joined the other kids on TV by cheering, "Kakie!"

Kakie, the Cake Monster, appeared on the screen. The monster was an overgrown puppet, with a super-sweet voice. He carried a huge cake. "Wheeee! Kakie one happy monster! Kakie love Cake! Yummy! Tummy get a tummy ache!"

Dennis laughed.

"Whoa, whoa, whoa." Dracula took a closer look at the TV. "How is that a monster?"

Kakie sang, "Have some cake, Wuzzlelumplebum!"

Wuzzlelumplebum, another cute animal-like monster, ate some cake and made a funny noise to say it was delicious.

"Remember, kids, a real monster always shares!" Kakie said.

"Shares . . . yes! When I think monsters—I think shares!" Dracula rolled his eyes. Kakie was insane. He turned to Dennis and said, "Now, let me tell you what a real monster is, Denisovich—"

Dennis looked confused.

"Dad, please. He's practically five already. Don't force it." Mavis sang Dennis a lullaby. *"Twinkle, twinkle little star, how I wonder what you are . . ."*

Dennis yawned. "I'm too old for lullaby . . ."

Dracula didn't listen to him. Mavis's song was odd. "What? That's not how that one goes."

"This is the way most people sing it," Mavis explained.

"Most people? What's wrong with 'Suffer, suffer, scream in pain, blood is spilling from your brain'?" He sang the words the way he always did.

"Daddy . . . ," Mavis interrupted.

"Come on, you . . . you know how I sang it to you." He sang out, "Zombies . . ." And Mavis joined in, ". . . gnaw you like a plum, piercing cries, and you succumb."

When they stopped, Dennis was fast asleep.

Dracula finished the serenade on his own. "Suffer, suffer, scream in pain, you will never breathe again." He looked at Mavy, and just like Dennis, she was also asleep.

CHAPTER FIVE

Out in the woods the wolf pups played. There were so many pups, and they were so wild, they destroyed everything in their path.

A group of monster friends watched as a few wolf pups went to play in a bouncy house. Other pups were fighting with sticks at the dog fort clubhouse while more were gnawing wildly on a tire swing. A zombie was trying to entertain the pups by making balloon animals, but he struggled to keep anyone's attention as dozens of pups tore a piñata to shreds nearby.

"Ohhh, aren't they sweet?" Wanda asked, watching her babies play.

"Yeah. There's a reason they call it a litter," Wayne agreed.

Dracula was thrilled when he saw Mavis come in with Dennis.

"Happy birthday, Wally, Wilson, Wade, Whoopi, Waylon, and Weepy!" Dennis shouted.

"Denisovich! My big boy!" Dracula swept the boy up into a hug, then said to Mavis, "You made it!"

"I'm just trying this for you, Dad," she said.

Dracula kissed Mavis. "Thank you, Coffin Cake."

Suddenly Winnie, now six years old herself, jumped on Dennis and hugged him, knocking him down. "Dennis! I love you! Zing!"

"Hi, Winnie!" Dennis squirmed out from under her.

"I just love your yummy strawberry locks. Zing. Zing!" Winnie pulled Dennis's curly hair and then flipped him judo style.

"You like our house fort?" she asked, leaning over his flushed face and pointing at the clubhouse.

"It's pretty cool," Dennis said, trying to squirm free again.

"Good, because that's where we're gonna live when

we get married!" Winnie started licking Dennis's face. Wanda dashed in and spritzed her with a spray bottle.

"Winnie?" Wanda said kindly. "Give him his space, hon. I'm sorry, Mavis." Wanda pulled Winnie off Dennis.

"It's okay, Aunt Wanda, we just stopped by to say happy birthday, 'cause the sun's gonna come out and we gotta get to classes." Mavis moved to go.

"What? We're just about to play musical chairs!" Dracula blocked the way.

Johnny was willing to stay longer. "Oh, he can do that."

Dennis finally broke free from Winnie. "Yay!"

Mavis looked concerned as Dennis joined the pups around a circle of chairs, waiting for the music to start. Suddenly the pups started demolishing the chairs as gentle music played. They smashed the chairs over each other's heads and turned into a Tasmanian Devil tornado of wild pups.

Dennis was having the best time of his life!

As the pups got more and more crazy, Dennis was thrown out of the circle and landed by the zombie clown. Wolf pups ran over, grabbed Dennis, and put his mouth on the clown's helium tank. He immediately started floating. The wolf pups hit him back and forth with tennis rackets.

"Dennis!" Mavis shouted.

"Relax, Mavis, the kids play like this all the time. They're perfectly fine," Wanda assured her.

"Yeah, we made sure they ran around before the party to burn off that extra energy," Wayne said.

Mavis was trying desperately to follow the frantic action. "Now where did they go?"

Dennis and other kids were riding on the backs of several wolf pups, having a race around the trees.

A cat accidentally wandered into the middle of the race. The pup carrying Dennis started to chase to the cat. He ran through some trees. Dennis was lifted off the back of the pup by some other pups hanging in the trees. They started to swing him, Tarzan style, through the trees.

He grabbed a swinging rope and launched himself off. Dennis landed in the bouncy house. Some pups rushed in and Dennis was wildly bounced from floor to ceiling and wall to wall. A yeti kid jumped real high on one end, popping the house and causing Dennis to fly through the air. . . . He landed on a towering pile of presents. He barely kept his balance on the swaying mountain, but managed to climb to the top. He raised his arm for victory, but just then more pups charged in to destroy the mountain. They sent Dennis careening off. Mavis rushed to save him, but he landed headfirst in the pups' birthday cake.

The pups surrounded the cake, devouring it in seconds. They ran off, with a few still licking the frosting off Dennis as he giggled from the tickles of their tongues.

Finally, Mavis was able to grab him.

"Dennis! Are you okay?" Mavis asked her baby.

"Ya! Best. Party. Ever." He smiled at his mom to reveal he was missing a tooth!

"Little dude! Your tooth came out!" Johnny was so proud.

"What? Are you kidding me? You got your tooth knocked out?" Mavis was horrified.

But Dracula was thrilled. "Oh, yes indeed! Here comes the fang!"

"Dad, his baby tooth wasn't a fang, why would this one be? He's not a monster. He can't be doing what the other monster kids are doing." She sighed. Dennis and the monster kids were sometimes too much for her to handle. She brought her son in close and started putting Corpserstone sunscreen on him—SPF 10,000.

"Sweetheart, he lives here. He's gonna be around stuff like this. He has to get used to it," Dracula said, trying to calm her down.

"Well, maybe he doesn't," she countered.

"What are you saying?" Dracula stopped what he was doing to stare at her.

"We've been talking about moving," Mavis admitted. "Somewhere safer for Dennis. I'm sorry. But you just can't make somebody something they're not!"

She took Dennis and tried to leave the party. Winnie cried. "Zing. Zing!"

Dracula followed them out. "Mavy, wait! You can't mean that." He caught Johnny nearby and pulled him over. "You're in on this? The leaving?"

He nervously reported, "It's not definite at all. It's just something she's definitely talking about, but until we do it . . . it's not definitive."

Dracula gave him an unhappy look as Johnny rushed off to be with Mavis and Dennis.

After he left, Johnny felt something crunchy in his hair. "Did he just cover me with birdseed?" It was a cruel prank. A hundred birds attacked Johnny, picking at his hair and clothing. Johnny flipped his arms, trying to get them off. "Yeah. He covered me."

Obviously Dracula was mad at Johnny.

Dracula went back to the castle to talk to his wife. He stood in front of her portrait and said, "Am I really going to lose them, Martha?" He glanced at a painting of Mavs, Johnny, and Dennis that hung next to Martha's. "I don't think I could bear it if they left me. I'd feel so alone. I know the boy's got it in him. I know I can get those fangs out of him. What am I going to do?"

Feeling deeply sad, he crawled into his coffin. "I can't lose the only family I have—" Dracula felt something in his coffin and jumped up. "Gaaaah!"

Johnny revealed himself. He was hiding under the

blankets. "Where's Mavis? Is she around?"

"What? No! How'd you get under there?" Dracula nearly fell back as Johnny hugged him. He couldn't let go, no matter how hard Dracula tried to shake him off.

"What are we going to do, Drac?! I don't wanna leave! I love it here!" Johnny wailed.

Dracula managed to flip Johnny onto the ground. "Well, tell that to my daughter!"

Johnny gave Dracula an insane look. "I did! She's not listening! All she's talking about is going to my hometown to see if it's a good place for Dennis to live."

Dracula asked, "And what did you say?"

"Well, I know I turned out pretty cool, but believe me, it was a lot of hard work to get this way. I mean, you met my family." Johnny waved a finger around his ear in big circles that indicated "crazy."

"Yes, and I have to say I've never seen that many stiffs outside of a crypt before," Dracula joked.

Johnny didn't laugh. "Drac, my dad's gonna want me to get a job! At his office! I don't even know what he does! But you have to wear shoes!" Johnny started crying. He glanced down at his dirty old tennis shoes.

"You're my bestest kicks! Don't ever leave my feet!"

"Okay, okay. Stop talking to your sneakers." There had to be a solution. "Let me think . . . If I could just get some alone time with Denisovich, I could teach him how to be a real monster."

"But what if he isn't a monster?" Dennis tossed out.

Dracula raised his voice. "He is a monster! He's just a late fanger."

The shrunken head by the door said, "He turns five next week. If he's not a vampire by his birthday, it ain't happening."

"Oh, it ain't ain't happening, baby." Dracula was certain. "Here's the plan: You go away with Mavis to your parents' house. Don't make it too good, of course, but let her have fun so she's not thinking about what I'm doing with Denisovich."

"Which is . . . what?" Johnny asked.

Dracula had a plan. "While you're away with Mavis, me and the boys will take Dennis to all our old haunts! Each of us will show him our monster skills, and he'll be fanging it up in no time!"

Dracula imagined teaching Dennis how to catch a

mouse, and Dennis happily gaining confidence as his missing tooth turned into a huge fang. Another huge fang would knock out his other baby tooth.

"I'm calling the guys!" Dracula pulled out his smartphone and struggled to dial it. "D-aaaahhhh!"

Dracula's shrunken head chuckled. "Cut them nails, kitty cat!"

"Shut up!" Dracula told the head. He wasn't in the mood.

CHAPTER SIX

Mavis and Johnny took a shiny black hearse to the airport. Before they got into the car, Johnny gave Dennis a good-bye hug.

Mavis told her father the details for the weekend. "So it's sliced avocado, rolled oats with apricot, the Aveeno moisturizer after every bath, and—"

"And then the shea butter on his tush before his pj's. And then twenty minutes with the nebulizer while I read his Learning Factory Phonics book to him." Dracula finished the list.

"And you remember how to video chat?" Mavis asked.

Dracula waved her away. "Yes, yes, with the phone and the buttons and the agony."

Mavis smiled. "Thanks for trying so hard, Dad. I know you'll keep him safe."

"Of course, Mavy. Stake my heart and hope to die," Dracula said.

"I'm just gonna miss him," Mavis said. She pulled her son in for a hug. "Love you, Dennis."

"I love you, Mommy!" Dennis said.

"I'll tell him Mavy Wavy stories every night before bed," Dracula told her.

Mavis jumped into her father's arms. "You're the best. I love you, Dad."

Johnny also hugged Dracula. "Gonna miss all you guys! You're all my family. Love you, Drac!"

Dracula dragged himself away. "Yes, yes . . . with the love." He slipped over to Johnny and whispered, "Remember the plan. Just keep her distracted and happy. But not too happy. Capiche?"

"Got it," Johnny said. "Operation Just Keep Her Distracted and Happy, But Not Too Happy, Capiche starts now. Cool?"

Dracula winked. And Johnny said more loudly, "Will you hug my backpack?"

"No." Dracula refused.

Johnny and Mavis got in the hearse and drove away.

Dennis reached up for Dracula. "Mmmm . . . back to bed."

Dracula said, "Uh, yes, we'll get to the bed, we all love the bed. But we're just gonna do one thing first . . ."

Just then, another hearse pulled up. Frankenstein, Wayne, Murray, and Griffin rushed out of the hotel and toward the hearse. They were all carrying lots of luggage.

"Is it shorts weather where we're going?" Frankenstein asked.

"Geez, I hope not, I woulda packed my ankle socks," Murray said.

Moments later Dracula and the monsters and Dennis were all packed into the hearse.

"How do you click in this stupid car seat?" he complained as he struggled with the fasteners on Dennis's seatbelt.

"You gotta cut those nails, man," Frankenstein said.

"We just strap our kids down with duct tape," Wayne said.

Dracula caught sight of the Blob through the window. He was headed for the hearse.

"What's he doing here?" Dracula asked.

"I told him he could come. He's never been outside the hotel," Frankenstein said.

Dracula had to stop this! "Blob, there's no room! Sorry, man!"

"Glurrbleebloo." The Blob squashed himself into the car, smashing everyone together.

Murray could barely breathe. "Yeah, that ain't happening."

Dracula's muffled voice mumbled, "Fine, put him on the Rascal. Let's just get going."

The zombie bellmen hooked up a Rascal scooter to the side of the hearse, and the Blob slid on. The hearse took off quickly. The Blob nearly slipped off but rode alongside with the scooter like a sidecar.

"Where we going, Papa Drac?" Dennis asked, looking out the window.

"Oh, Denisovich, we're going to have an adventure! A monstery adventure!" Dracula clapped his hands, building the excitement.

"Yay! Monsters! We're gonna eat cake!" Dennis cheered.

"What'd he say?" Wayne didn't understand.

"No, no cake on this monster trip!" Dracula told Dennis.

"No cake cebause Kakie says too much cake makes tummy ache! Yay! A monster always shares!" Dennis recited what he'd learned on TV.

"Wow." Griffin's glasses seemed to stare at Dennis.

"We may need more than a week," Wayne said.

"Hey, you know who could fix the kid in a snap?" Frankenstein had a great idea. "Vlad."

Dracula protested. "What? We don't need to call Vlad." He told his friends, "We got this." Putting a hand on Dennis's arm, Dracula explained, "Eh, you see, Denisovich, monsters are nice, just like you . . . but when the moon comes out, the real monster fun begins—being scary! Right, guys?"

On the radio, a fresh pop song began, and instead of

answering Dracula, everyone began singing.

"Guys! Guys!" Dracula shut off the radio. "What is wrong with you?"

"Come on, everybody likes that song," Frankenstein told Dracula, to stop him from being such a fun-killer.

"We're not everybody! We're scary monsters, remember?" Dracula put a CD into the car's player.

"Hey, what are you putting in?" Griffin asked.

"It's an audio book. Bigfoot's life story. He reads it himself." Dracula was satisfied with his pick. It was far more appropriate for their mission.

"Grrrrrhhhhh.... Rrrrhhnnngggghhh...."

The growling went on and on. Dennis fell back to sleep.

Outside, on the scooter, the Blob was still happily listening to the pop song on his headphones.

CHAPTER SEVEN

The Air Transylvania plane landed on a runway in Santa Cruz, California. Johnny and Mavis gathered their stuff and rented a car.

"Gotta admit, it's cool that we're all here together," Johnny said as he loaded their suitcases into the trunk.

"All?" Mavis asked.

"Yeah, me and you and my backpack." He glanced through an open window. "Are ya comfy back there, buddy?"

The backpack was resting on the backseat with a seatbelt on.

For a long moment Mavis marveled at the mountains

outside, but then she checked her phone. Then, back to the mountains. "Wow. This is gonna be amazing."

"Yeah . . . amazing, but not that amazing." Johnny was thinking about the plan he'd made with Dracula. "Capiche?"

"Uh . . . not exactly," Mavis said.

Johnny shared a nervous look with the backpack.

"I want to see everything you did growing up!" Mavis told him.

"Yeah? You wanna see how your husband became the Earl of Awesome he is today?"

Mavis giggled.

"Sure, we can even hit a few spots on the way to my parents,'" Johnny told her.

"Lemme just quickly call home. . . ." Mavis pulled out her phone again.

"Whoa . . . it's only one a.m. there. Dennis isn't even up yet." Johnny had to slow her down.

"Right. I'm sorry, Johnny." Mavis put away the phone. "I'm just not used to being away from him."

"Everything's gonna be cool," Johnny assured her. "Your dad was so all over it!"

"I know," Mavis agreed. "That's why I love my dad. He's the best!"

Dracula directed Griffin to turn onto a dirt road. Dennis was napping. His head bounced from the bumps.

"Right, turn here." Dracula pointed the way. It was time to wake his grandson. "Denisovich, rise and shine! Boys, this bringing back any memories? Boys?"

The monsters in the backseat, Frankenstein, Murray and Wayne, were all watching a funny video on a phone.

"Guys! Put that away!" Dracula needed them to pay attention. "Enough!" With a swoop of his cape, Dracula pointed to where they were. "Don't you remember this? We used to prowl around here when we were in our hundreds! The Dark Forest of Slobozia!"

The dirt road ended at neatly manicured park. Some late-night, dog-walking humans were exercising, wearing yoga pants, and chatting under the bright street lamps.

Dennis giggled.

Dracula was disgusted.

But Frankenstein was impressed. "Nice how they built it up."

"Okay, out of the car!" Dracula opened his door. "Denisovich. You're going to see every monster do his specialty. First, Frank's gonna show us how he scares people!"

"Yay!" Dennis followed Frank into the park. "He's gonna say, 'Boo!'"

"Yeah, I don't think 'boo' has ever worked." Dracula shook his head. "But that's why we're here: to learn from the master!"

"'Kay, I'll give it a shot." Frankenstein stretched as he got ready. A couple of joggers ran by.

They recognized him. "Hey! Frankenstein!" one jogger shouted.

"Hey, how you doin'?" Frank asked.

The other jogger said, "You're awesome! Can we take a picture? Is that okay?"

"Sure," Frankenstein agreed. He got into the shot. "Okay . . . little selfie action?"

"For real?" Dracula moaned.

The first jogger selfied a picture of them. Frankenstein

placed his head in between them and made a goofy face.

"Ha-ha. Awesome," the jogger said. "Thank you so much!"

"Have a great day!" With a friendly wave, Frankenstein walked away.

Dennis wanted to scare people his own way. "Boo!" he shouted at the joggers.

"Oh . . . he's adorable!" the joggers gushed.

"Adorable. Yes. Okay." Dracula encouraged Dennis. "Not scary, but 'boo' is a start."

Dennis's hair popped out, extra curly, making him even more adorable.

Dracula loaded everyone back into the car and took them to a darker, more woodsy area of the park.

Dennis talked the whole way. "And my birthday cake's gonna have the coolest guy on it! He climbs walls and wears a cape!"

"Oh really, and who is this very cool guy?" Dracula asked.

"Batman!" Dennis announced.

Dracula asked, "Batman? Great. You don't know anyone else with a cape that's cool?" He swished his cape, but Dennis didn't notice. Dracula gave up. "This is good. Stop here!"

Griffin parked the car, and they all climbed out of the hearse.

"Okay, Wayne, it's your turn," Dracula said. "Go kill something." He picked up Dennis. "Denisovich, watch this."

"What?" Wayne asked.

"I told you! Come on! If we don't inspire Denisovich, how's he going to find his inner monster?" Dracula was getting frustrated. This was not going as planned.

"Papa, who's in a monster?" Dennis asked, wrinkling his nose.

"Whuh?" Dracula remembered what he'd told Wayne. "No, no, your *inner* monster."

"Why can't we just call Vlad?" Wayne asked, turning his back toward the woods.

"Vlad's not gonna happen," Dracula insisted.

"But Vlad's way always works," Murray said.

Dracula ended the conversation "I don't wanna hear any more about Vlad."

"What's a Vlad?" Dennis asked, curious.

"Nothing." Dracula opened the bag Mavis had packed. "Just, here, have an avocado."

"Yay!" Dennis licked his lips.

"Your mommy says it's 'good fat'! Whatever the heaven that means." Dracula dug through Dennis's tote bag and handed him an avocado, which Dennis peeled and sliced by himself.

Dennis showed Frankenstein the slices, offering some. Frank took the pit in the middle and chewed it.

"Listen. I'm not killing any people." Wayne was over that. "I'm not gonna set monsters back again just to make your kid like vampires. Anyway, there's nothing to kill here! It's all been—"

A deer crossed nearby. Dracula glared at Wayne.

"Awwwww . . . what a cutie," Frank gushed.

Dracula glared at Frankenstein.

"But we should kill him," Frankenstein said quickly.

"Great. You know, I haven't done this in years. We don't need to kill anymore. We have Pop Tarts." Wayne was not interested. Not at all.

It didn't matter to Dracula. "Denisovich, you're going to love this. Wayne's going to eat that whole deer. And the next one's yours. Wayne, go!"

Wayne approached the deer, who glanced at him sweetly.

"Oh man . . . I'm too old for this," Wayne moaned. "Okay . . . how's it go again? Ow-ooo? No, that's for the moon. I growl. Here goes . . . Growl!" Wayne took off toward the deer.

Dracula smiled. It was a start.

Suddenly a Frisbee flew over the deer. A voice shouted, "Get it, boy!"

Wayne instinctively started to bark and wildly chased the Frisbee. He snagged it in the air, fighting off another dog. The man looked puzzled. So did the deer. Dracula couldn't believe what just happened.

Dennis clapped. "Yay! Uncle Wayne got the Frisbee."

When they left the park, Dracula was mad. Wayne was still holding the Frisbee in his mouth.

"Some werewolf. Did you actually say the word 'growl'? You're a werewussy." Dracula couldn't hold back his anger.

"I said I was rusty!" Wayne explained, talking with the disc in his mouth.

"Gimme that Frisbee!" Dracula grabbed for it.

"No, it's my Frisbee. I fetched it!" Wayne pulled back.

They struggled for the Frisbee over Griffin, who was driving.

"Hey! Whoa!" Griffin swerved the car, then made a hard turn. The Blob's scooter separated as it flew off the road. Everyone watched with horror as the scooter flew over a cliff.

"He'll be fine. He's blobby," Dracula said at last.

CHAPTER EIGHT

It was a warm night with soft ocean breezes in Santa Cruz. Johnny and Mavis were driving down a beautiful street.

"This place is so amazing and scenic!" Mavis cooed, looking between the tall trees and the quaint houses. "What do you want to show me first?" she asked Johnny.

"Mmm . . . I dunno, it's pretty, but there's really nothing to do once it gets dark. Ooh . . . You wanna see the playground where I got my first concussion?" Johnny turned a corner.

"Yes!" Mavis said, but then got distracted. "Wait—what's that place?"

Johnny slowed the car in front of the minimart. A few moments later they'd parked and gone inside.

Mavis was looking through bags of potato chips. She asked the cashier, "So you're telling me that I can pick between all these different kinds of chips?"

"Yes," the cashier told her.

"How do people decide?" Mavis was overwhelmed. The cashier shrugged.

"Whoa! Now, what's that beautiful fountain of rubies?"

Mavis got a cup and filled it with the ruby red slush. She downed it in one gulp.

"Johnny! Have you tried this Slurpay?"

"Not . . . that quickly, hon," Johnny warned. But Mavis was already onto the next flavor.

"It comes in forty-eight flavors! We have to try them all!" She immediately refilled her cup.

"Uh, I don't know if we have time," Johnny said, watching her gulp that one down and refill again.

"Why? This place is open all night!" She finished the third slush drink and asked the cashier, "Right, sir?"

"Yes," the man assured her.

Twenty minutes later Johnny was still standing at the cashier, patiently waiting. "You know, we still haven't seen my favorite bungee golf courses," Johnny said.

Mavis sat on the counter, surrounded by a few dozen empty Slurpay cups. She was scratching off a lottery ticket with a quarter.

"Oh, Johnny, this place is so much fun . . . you're so lucky, Kal!" Mavis grinned. Her teeth were completely rainbow colored.

"Yes." Kal, the cashier, was drinking Slurpays with her. His teeth were glowing bright colors.

Mavis read the lottery ticket. "Try again!" She was excited. "Johnny, I get to try again!"

"Awesome." Johnny sighed. He was stuck in the minimart, and there was no end in sight.

"What you want me to do now?" Murray, the Mummy, asked Dracula.

"Denisovich, you won't believe it!" Dracula was glad it was finally Murray's turn to impress the boy. "The Mummy can crash through walls and turn into a swarm of beetles and put a curse on anyone!"

Dennis frowned. "That sounds mean!"

"It's fun-mean!" Dracula told him. "Okay. So, check it out—Murray's going to conjure up the biggest sandstorm you've ever seen! Hit it!"

"Sandstorm? It's been a while." Murray considered how to start.

"Not my problem. Do it. Say your little spell," Dracula encouraged.

"Okay, I got this," Murray said. "Frank, Wayne, just try not to faint, 'cause I'm bringing it down hardcore."

Murray waved his arms and chanted, with dramatic Egyptian pantomiming. As the others watched, Dennis was working hard to copy his moves.

Suddenly Murray twisted wrong and fell to the ground in pain. "Oh! My back!"

A tiny sandstorm brewed above them. The sand swirled in a small tornado, then dropped in front of Murray, leaving a small pile. Dennis rushed in and quickly made a sand snowman. Frank finished it off by putting one of Dennis's carrots on for a nose, and they all laughed.

Except for Dracula.

In Santa Cruz, Johnny had gotten Mavis to leave the minimart. They were in the car again, when Mavis spotted some kids riding BMX-type bikes in a brightly lit park.

"Wait! Stop at that playground! Look at these cute kids! Holy rabies!" Mavis said, seeing their tricks. "This looks like a blast!"

"I dunno, Mavy, this can be pretty dangerous if you don't know what you're doing." Johnny's face went from serious to a huge grin. "Of course, I rock these bikes. May I, little dude?"

The kid shrugged and passed over his bike.

Johnny put on a helmet that was way too small for him. A second later he was doing cool tricks on a bike that was also ridiculously small.

"Check it out!" he called to his wife. "Oh yeah! This is how I rolled every summer!"

Mavis giggled. The kids clapped.

He skidded the bike to a stop near Mavis. "Okay, let's see what you got, babe!"

"Wow. . . . I'll give it a try. . . ." Mavis was a little nervous.

The helmet and bike fit her better than Johnny. She started out wobbly but gradually got the hang of it, until she was doing amazing moves. The kids gasped. She did a loop-de-loop without ever touching ground, pedals upside down, and finally froze in midair. After a few moments of stunned silence . . .

"Ya feel me now?! That's my girlfriend, suckers!" Johnny was so proud.

"Your wife, Johnny," Mavis reminded him.

"My wife! Even better!" He was more proud.

Mavis came down from midair, parked, and took off the helmet.

A kid came rushing up to her. "That was awesome! Where'd you learn how to do that stuff?"

"Transylvania," Mavis said.

"That's cool," the kid told her. "I have a cousin from Philadelphia."

"These kids are so sweet," Mavis said to Johnny. "Dennis would love them!"

"Sweet today, punks tomorrow," Johnny told her.

"We should hit my folks' place. I said we'd be there by now."

"Sure!" She looked at her watch. "Oh, hey, it's after three in Transylvania—I'm gonna check on Dennis, okay?"

In Transylvania, Dennis was sound asleep on Dracula's lap. Frankenstein was eating a large fruit roll-up from Dennis's snack bag.

"Let's see . . . I have a *B* . . . Bangladesh," Wayne said. They were playing car games on the long ride.

"Okay, Bangladesh ends in *H*. I have an *H*. Honduras," Griffin said on his turn.

"Oh, that's a good one, Griffin," Murray said.

"Thank you," Griffin said. "Okay, Drac. It's your turn. You have an *S*."

"Suck it," Dracula said.

"Suck it? Where's that?" Murray asked.

Frankenstein said, "I don't think that's a place."

Dracula's phone rang. "Oh no . . . oh no no no . . . it's Mavis!"

"You gotta answer it," Wayne said.

Dracula was struggling with his fingernails again.

"You're pushing too hard. Lighter!" Murray instructed.

"All right! Denisovich, wake up." Dracula shook Dennis, but he didn't wake.

"Oh boy, he's out cold."

"I got this!" Griffin took over. He put his sunglasses on Dennis and propped him up, ready for the video chat.

Dracula managed to answer the phone.

Mavis saw a signal on her video chat, and then Dracula appeared on the screen.

"Dad! What took so long?" Mavis asked.

Dracula was holding the phone close so that Mavis couldn't see he was in a car.

"What? Nothing, Mavy! We're all great here at the hotel. Just doing hotel things. How are you?"

Mavis was glad to hear it. She said, "We're having a blast. We just went biking and minimarting. It's so fun here! Is Dennis okay?"

"Of course! You want to see him?" Dracula checked that Griffin had him ready.

"Yes! Yes, I do!" Mavis was eager.

Dracula turned the phone to show Dennis.

"Hi, baby! How are you?" Mavis asked in her sweetest voice.

Griffin moved Dennis's arms like a puppet, making it appear he was awake. Griffin also imitated Dennis's voice. "Mommy! I happy!"

"Hey, little dude!" Johnny put his head in the frame.

"I wish you were here, buddy! You would love it so much!" Johnny said, then asked, "Why is he wearing sunglasses?"

"Oh, we were playing . . . it's a superhero thing!" Dracula said quickly.

"Oh, okay. Which one, honey?" Mavis asked.

"Uh . . . I'm Sunglasses Man!" Griffin didn't have a better idea.

"Oh, ho . . . you're so cute," Mavis told him.

"Cebause I'm Sunglasses Man to the rescue! I'm flying!" Griffin tipped Dennis like a plane. He looked like he was trying to fly.

Dracula whispered to Griffin, "Okay, take it down a notch."

"You sound funny." Mavis wrinkled her brow.

"Oh, no no, that's his Sunglasses Man voice. He's been doing it all night." Dracula faked a bad signal. "Chhhhh . . . static, the signal is bad. Chhhh . . . chhhhhh . . . Mavis, are you there? Static . . . static."

Mavis shook her phone. "Yeah, I'm still—" But the call ended. Dracula and Dennis disappeared from the screen.

Mavis told Johnny, "All right, I'll stop worrying. I guess he's having fun."

"Course he is," Johnny said, and Mavis sighed with relief.

"Well, I nailed it with the Sunglasses Man! Right off the top of my head. I threw in a 'cebause'—did everyone see that?" Griffin asked. It was too bad no one could see his big grin.

"She said she was having fun!" Dracula was so unhappy with the way it was turning out. "Johnny's blowing it.

She's biking and minimarting and wishing he was there. She's gonna wanna move!"

He glared at Dennis's mouth. "Holy rabies. No sign of fangotry! We gotta fix this kid! Okay, enough of you guys teaching him. Time for me to show him where a vampire learns!"

Out of desperation, Dracula pulled out his cell phone again. Then he turned to his friends. "Someone turn on the navigator on this thing."

Murray manipulated the navigator, saying, "Look how light I touch it."

"Please enter your destination! Pleeease! I'm begging you!" the navigator voice said.

The hearse began to follow the route.

CHAPTER NINE

"Yeah. This is gonna be good, Denisovich. Scary stuff. Okay? It's in you. We just gotta concentrate on the scary." He wanted to stay focused.

"Papa Drac, do you miss Grandma?" Dennis asked, out of the blue.

"Miss Grandma?" Dracula was thrown off. "Oh, sure I do. I miss her every day. She was my zing. Why do you ask?"

"I don't know." Dennis got unusually quiet.

"Do you miss anybody?" Dracula asked.

"I miss Mommy and Daddy," Dennis said sadly.

"And who else? You miss that Winnie?" Dracula

asked. "The pup who tackles you and tries to lick you all the time?"

"Yeah. But we're just friends," Dennis answered.

Dracula laughed to himself. "Sure, that's how it always starts."

The GPS navigator interrupted in a creepy, tense voice. "Right turn! Now! Here! You imbecile!"

"Oh, right! Turn, Griffin!" Dracula instructed.

"Yes, Papa Drac," Griffin said.

"Wait and see, fellas, this kid'll be guzzling goat blood in no time." Dracula felt certain he had it all under control.

"You have arrived at your destination! Yes! YES!" The navigator was happy to have gotten them to the forest.

"Here we are! It's the Vampire Summer Camp I went to as a kid!" He looked at the small tents set up in the woods. Dracula was flooded with memories.

Little vampire kids were everywhere, running and playing.

"You see, Denisovich, this is where I learned to catch mice and shape shift and use my incredible powers and strength! Pretty cool, huh?" Dracula was certain Dennis was going to fit right in . . . quickly, too.

"Badminton!" Dennis saw a bunch of vampire kids playing.

Looking at the kids playing badminton made Dracula curious. He looked around, and every activity appeared to be harmless. Some kids were playing tetherball, others were singing. Seriously. Singing.

"Yes. I don't remember this badminting," Dracula said softly, considering what had happened to the camp.

Suddenly the camp director, a young, new-age vampire with a gentle voice, approached. "Well, well, is this a night? Hey, how ya doin', folks, I'm Dana, the director. Welcome to Camp Winnepacaca."

"I told you," Wayne said.

"We're sure excited to have the Count visiting us. He made quite a name for himself around here back in the day," Dana said to Dracula.

"Well, I suppose I was always a bit special." Dracula was embarrassed to be singled out.

"Oh, that's putting it mildly. You folks should see his old bunk," Dana told the monsters.

"What? Oh, that's not necessary," Dracula said, but then was dragged along to the bunkhouse. Inside the darkened cabin, Dana opened a tiny coffin with an enormous pee stain inside. Everyone was laughing—except Dracula.

"Yessir, that's a bigger landmark at camp than the flagpole," Dana told them.

"Papa Peepee!" Dennis laughed harder than anyone else.

"All right. Moving on. I'm very interested in sending my grandboy, Denisovich, here," Dracula said, ruffling the kid's hair.

"Oh! This little . . . red-headed . . . non-fangy lil' guy?" Dana was surprised.

"Oh, they're in there. Gonna grow in. He's a late fanger. That's why we came here. Can you show us some of the drills, like where they catch the mice?" Dracula asked.

"Can do. Course, now we call it tee-mousing." Dana led the group to the field house.

It was a beginning version of mice-eating. The mice were on a tee instead of being caught in the wild. The kids ran up one at a time and grabbed the mouse.

"So they don't have to catch the mice?" Dracula asked Dana.

"Nope. We find this is a good way to build their confidence." They all noticed that one kid was having trouble getting the mouse.

"It's right there!" Dracula shouted at the kid. "What's the matter with you?"

The kid gave Dracula a frightened look, then grabbed the mouse and ran away.

"Hokey pokey," Dana said with a small smile. A counselor brought out a big bowl of mice and the kids all reached into it and grabbed mice to eat. "Not too many! Remember, kids, a vampire always shares!"

Dracula rolled his eyes. "Again with the shares."

"You can have one, little guy." Dana dangled a mouse in front of Dennis. "Any allergies or color restrictions?"

"He can eat a mouse!" Dracula said firmly.

But alas, Dennis didn't want to.

Dracula needed another task. He looked around and saw a two-hundred-foot-tall rickety old diving tower. "Ah, there it is, Denisovich, where Papa learned to fly!"

"Ooh, I wanna fly like Papa!" Dennis said.

They headed that way, but the tower was roped off.

Dana explained, "Ah, yeah . . . we're over here now."

Vampire kids with instructors were lined up to jump off a four-foot-high tower. They were all wearing helmets and padding. A few jumped off and kept the padding on, even when they turned into bats.

"Had to scale it down. Insurance," Dana said with shrug.

The last vampire kid jumped and fell, swinging on a rope. He squealed, "Help me."

Dracula was silent and furious.

"Hokey pokey," Dana said, ready to move on. "See ya at the campfire?"

In California, Grampa Mike and Grandma Linda greeted Johnny and Mavis as they arrived.

"Well, gosh, welcome, you two," Grandma Linda said, stepping aside to let them in.

"Hey, gang." Grampa Mike welcomed them into the living room.

Mavis jumped in for hugs. "Hi, guys! This is so exciting!"

"Our castle is your castle. Just not as spooky!" Grandma Linda gave a small laugh.

"Oh, thanks! Wow! I can't believe I'm actually here!" Mavis looked around the room, eagerly exploring their house.

"Well, you are! Now, how does it work, are you up all night, and sleep all day? Or can you join us for breakfast, like people would?" Grandma Linda asked Mavis.

"Yeah . . . ," Johnny started, but Mavis was so enthusiastic to be there she added, "Oh, I'll do whatever you guys want. I can try to sleep later tonight."

"Good! 'Cause I bought this pretty sunhat for you . . ." Grandma Linda gave Mavis a huge sunhat with a dark veil hanging off it, and a poncho.

"Linda—" Mike began.

"And I have a sunhat, but otherwise this poncho if you want to be safe." Grandma Linda thought it was a good gift.

"We can deal with it later, Linda," Mike said.

"Okay. Oh! Come see, I've set up your bedroom."

Linda opened a door and revealed her guest room makeover. She'd set it up complete with Halloween decorations and a makeshift coffin. "Monster Mash" was playing. Mavis and Johnny stood there in complete shock.

"I'm sorry... is that...?" Mavis pointed to the coffin.

"We didn't have a lot of time, so we just converted our poolside storage bin," Linda said.

"Less is more, Linda," Mike told her.

"It's... just like Transylvania." Mavis tried to sound positive.

"Oh, Transylvania. That was a fun experience. Mike was afraid he'd get disemboweled and eaten, and I told him he was just being silly." Linda gave an awkward laugh.

"That was you, Linda," Mike said. He wasn't laughing.

"But now we're so happy you're all thinking about moving to Santa Cruz!" Linda said.

Mavis took it all in, coffin and all. "I love it here! What an awesome place to raise a kid..."

That was bad for Johnny. "Oh, I don't know about 'awesome.' Maybe 'tubular'... but that's being way too generous..."

The doorbell rang.

"Oh, there they are. You know, we have a couple of mixed families in the neighborhood, so I thought I'd invite them over. They might be nice for you guys to talk to." Linda hurried off to welcome her guests.

Grandma Linda entered the living room with two couples. Caren and Pandragora entered first. Pandragora was a freaky-looking but mellow monster with a surfer dude accent.

"Hi, Caren. Hi, Pandragora," Linda greeted them.

"Welcome, Mavis!" Caren greeted Mavis warmly.

Pandragora said, "Hey, guys." As he spoke, he casually grabbed flying insects from the air and ate them. "Yeah, you're gonna dig it here!" He put his arm around Caren. "Don't even worry, people are totally cool with the intermarriage thing."

Caren said to Mavis, "I mean, the kids get picked on, but it toughens them up."

The next couple entered the living room. Loretta and Paul were Linda and Mike's neighbors. Paul was super hairy, with a scraggly beard.

"Oh, hey, you guys! And this is Loretta, she's married

to Paul, who's a werewolf," Linda told Johnny and Mavis.

"Excuse me?" Paul wrinkled his forehead, making his two eyebrows into one.

"Yes," Linda said cheerfully. "I was telling Mavis about the other monster-human couples in town."

"I am not a werewolf," Paul insisted.

"Oh . . . I thought . . ." Linda shrugged. "Well, you're welcome to stay and have some cupcakes!"

Paul turned and, with a bitter expression, left the house, dragging his wife with him.

"Anyone else?" She glanced out the front window to see if there were other guests coming. Then she held out a tray of cupcakes. "I made them special for Mavis."

The cupcakes were frosted in creepy, monstery designs.

Mavis smiled politely.

"I asked all the kids in the neighborhood what their worst nightmares were!" Grandma Linda said proudly, showing off the cupcake decorations.

CHAPTER TEN

That night at camp all the little vampire kids were sitting around in the glow of the firelight and singing. Dana played guitar.

"Vampire kids
Vampires will be friends forever
Through the centuries together
Even in the brightest sunny weather
Vampires will be friends forever
Lit-er-al-ly forever!"

The kids all shouted together, "Yay!"

Dana set aside the guitar. "Great job, vampires,

give yourselves a nice, big hug!"

As the kids hugged themselves, Murray and Frankenstein sat in the circle, hugging themselves, too.

Dracula nudged them. "We're going."

But Frankenstein was having such a good time. "What? Where?"

As they walked away, Dana started another song.

Dracula tried to block out the cheery music while he climbed the tall tower, holding Dennis. The others followed them up.

"Why are we doing this?" Murray asked, though Dracula had explained it a hundred times.

"You'd rather be listening to those putrid new songs? What happened to 'Michael, Row Your Corpse Ashore'? Or 'Kill-baya'?" Dracula grimaced.

Frank looked down from the tower. It was very high. "We shouldn't be up here, Drac."

"Who's ready to fly?" Dracula asked Dennis, ignoring his friends.

"Me! Me! Like a superhero!" Dennis shouted happily.

"Better! Like a vampire!" Dracula was encouraged. This was the right way to get the kid to transform. It was time for the big event. It was vampire time!

"This thing is rickety. Maybe the kid isn't supposed to fly," Frankenstein said as they reached the top of the tower. He looked down again and regretted it. The ground was very far away.

"Quiet! This is how they learn. You throw them and they figure it out. It's how I was taught! No one's ever got hurt from this." Dracula was ready.

"I wanna fly now!" Dennis said.

"Attabat!" Dracula held Dennis close. "You know Papa's right here if you need him!"

Griffin removed his glasses. "I can't watch this."

"Please don't," Murray begged.

"Here . . . we . . . go!" Dracula tossed his grinning grandson off the tower.

Everyone was horrified except for Dracula. He was thrilled.

"Wheeeeeeeeeee!" Dennis shrieked as he fell.

Dracula stayed calm.

The others were taking peeks . . . and freaking out.

"He's still not flying," Frankenstein said, his voice slightly panicked.

"He will," Dracula said.

Dennis's voice was getting softer as he fell farther and farther down the tower. "Wheeeeeee!"

"Still not," Wayne said with one eye open. The other, he covered in fear.

"It'll happen," Dracula said, his voice still confident.

The monsters heard a very faint, "Wheeee."

Frankenstein took a look at the ground. "This is a tall tower," he remarked.

"That's why it's good," Dracula said.

"You should get him," Murray insisted.

"He's gonna fall to his death," Wayne said.

"He's taking his time," Dracula said.

Dennis was now screaming.

"Drac!" Frank pointed at Dennis.

"I did that my first time," Dracula said, remembering when he was thrown off the tower himself.

More screaming.

All the monsters were scared, but not Dracula.

"He's getting too close to the ground," Murray warned.

Dennis kept screaming.

"You know what, he's not gonna fly," Dracula finally admitted.

He shot off the tower in a flash. As a bat, he swooped towards Dennis. Down below, the campers had abandoned the campfire and were gathered around, holding up their smartphones as they watched the fall.

Dracula swung in and caught Dennis exactly twelve inches from the ground. He did a loop-de-loop afterward and landed gracefully on the ground.

"I told you, Papa's always here for you," Dracula told Dennis.

"But I couldn't fly," Dennis said sadly.

"Hey, what can you do?" Dracula encouraged. "You're trying, my boy."

Dana frantically rushed up to them. "Oh dear. Oh my devil. We're gonna have to report this."

"You mean to the papers?" Dracula thought about it. "I guess it was pretty cool. But I'm not about getting press."

Dana shivered. "No, sir, I mean the authorities. I can't not report child endangerment."

Dracula put out a hand. "Whoa, listen to me! That was

fun!" He added, "Your singing is child endangerment."

The other monsters watched from the top of the tower.

"Should we go down and help him?" Wayne asked.

"Nope. I told him this was nuts. He's on his own." Frankenstein acted bored and leaned against the rail. The tower was so rickety, it started to lean with Frank's weight.

Down below, Dracula set Dennis down.

"We have to call the boy's mother," Dana said.

The tower was slowly starting to fall.

"What? No, that ain't happening. His mother's already nutsy cuckoo." Dracula tried to keep Dana away from the phone.

"I have to follow protocol," Dana said, showing the camp manual to Dracula.

Dracula tried to hypnotize him. "You will not follow protocol."

Dana blinked. "I'm a vampire. I can't be hypnotized."

Dracula shut off his hypno-eyes. "Oh. Right."

A large creak made Dracula and the campers look up. The tower was swaying back and forth. The monsters at the top were frantically looking for a quick exit.

"Now, please. Don't make me call the police," Dana told Dracula.

The camp kids started screaming as the tower began to tumble to the ground.

"No one's calling nobody!" Dracula stepped forward toward Dana when . . .

Suddenly the tower slammed to the ground. It landed right on the campfire!

Frank caught fire and ran around in flames as everyone scattered. Wayne and Murray rushed after him, trying desperately to get him to calm down. Frank ran around aimlessly, in and out of different camp buildings, setting them on fire as he went.

The kids all hurried forward, wanting a better view.

Dennis stayed behind with Dracula.

"Are we bad guys, Papa Drac?" Dennis asked.

"Bad? No, you're the best kid in the world. We didn't start the fire! It was that tower," Dracula said. Then he turned to Dana. "That's a very unsafe tower! You're lucky we don't call the authorities." He took Dennis by the hand. "Let's go, my hero!"

"Cebause I'm Batman!" Dennis flapped his arms like he could fly. "To the Batmobile!"

"Heh, yes, to the—"

Just then, flames hit the hearse, and the car blew up.

Mavis and Johnny sat together on the roof of Johnny's parents' home. The chorus of "Monster Mash" was coming from inside the house, playing on repeat.

"Sorry about all that stuff," Johnny said. "I guess they thought you'd like it."

"Why do I feel so weird here?" Mavis asked, staring out toward the ocean.

"No, hon, they're being weird," Johnny apologized.

"I think they're just trying to help me. I mean, I grew up knowing nothing, living inside that hotel. And you learned about everything, growing up in Santa Claus." Mavis was very forgiving.

"Santa Cruz, but, uh . . . ," Johnny started.

Mavis continued, "Maybe if Dennis grows up away from Transylvania, he won't be so freaky like me."

"Are you nuts, Mavis? You're a blast. You're so full

of life, and curious about everything. If Dennis grows up to be just like you, I'll be the luckiest dad in the world." Johnny put his arm around her shoulder.

She turned toward him. "I love you, Johnny Stein."

They began to kiss . . .

Mavis leaned back and looked into her husband's eyes. "You know what? As long as we're all together, we'll be happy anywhere. Even at the hotel."

Johnny gave a quiet "Yessss" before leaning in to kiss her again. Suddenly Johnny's phone buzzed. He glanced at the message.

"What are you doing?" Mavis asked.

"Whoa! Check out this video my friend sent me. This kid is an awesome daredevil!" He turned the phone toward Mavis.

The video was a little blurry, but it looked a lot like Dennis falling from a tower.

"Uh . . ." Johnny tried to pull back the phone.

"Wait! Is that Dennis?!" Mavis squinted at the little screen.

"No! Is it?" Johnny shook it off. "No! It's just, uh, hard to see . . ." He gave a small laugh and fumbled with the phone, pushing all the buttons at once. "Oops—just deleted it, so it's gone."

Mavis immediately dialed her own cell phone.

Sirens blared while the firemen tried to put out Frank's flames. Dracula heard a faint sound from his phone and took it out from under his cape.

"What? It's Mavis! I'm not answering it." He put down the phone.

"Come on, Drac, you have to," Frank said as the firefighters hosed him down.

"All right!" Dracula gave in. He answered, "Yes, honey bunch?"

"Dad, where are you?" Mavis asked.

"What? We're outside the hotel!" he lied. "Having a little cookout! It's perfectly safe!"

"What's that noise? Is that a siren?" Mavis knew he was up to something.

"Oh, those are just some wailing banshees checking in! Quiet, you banshees, we're trying to have a perfectly safe cookout over here!" Dracula put a hand over the phone to muffle the sound. Dennis started yelling.

"Mommy?! I wanna say hi!" He grabbed for the phone.

"Eh . . ." Dracula hesitated.

"Mommy, mommy!" Dennis shouted toward the receiver. "Papa Drac just tried to teach me how to—"

Dana came rushing over. "Is that the mother?"

In a panic, Dracula broke the phone on Dana's head, cracking the screen. He held what was left of the device away from his face, shaking it.

"Oh no! Static again!" He made throaty sounds. "Cchhhhhhh . . ."

"I am coming back to the hotel right now," Mavis told him. "And you better be there! Or I swear, Dad, you're gonna be very sorry!"

Mavis hung up the phone and immediately ran down the walls of the house, hyperventilating. Johnny followed her, but fell off the roof.

"What's going on?!" Johnny shouted at her as he brushed the leaves out of his hair.

"We need to get home right away!" Mavis told him.

"Okay. I'll go wake up my backpack!" Johnny rushed off, happy to be heading back to Transylvania.

CHAPTER ELEVEN

"Guys, we gotta move!" Dracula gathered his friends and Dennis. But then he realized, "We got no car. How we gonna get out of here?"

"Don't worry. I made a call," Griffin said.

Just then, the Blob pulled up on the Rascal scooter. He wasn't injured from the earlier crash, just covered with dirt and grass. That, and a stray squirrel was trapped in his body.

The Blob scolded them all in his blobby language.

"I'm sorry, Blob, we really meant to call you sooner!" Dracula said. He was the first to jump onto the scooter. "Hit it!"

Somehow the Blob was able to drive, though very awkwardly. Daylight was coming, so Dracula covered himself in his cloak and held on for the ride.

Mavis and Johnny were at the airport. They were desperate to get to the castle.

"Transylvania," Mavis told the ticket agent.

"You want to go where?" The agent's fingers hovered over her computer.

"Transylvania. As soon as possible," Mavis said.

"We don't fly direct to Transylvania," the ticket agent told her.

"You don't?" Mavis was surprised.

"You can go to Bucharest, but you'll have to switch planes in Chicago, and then Zurich." She looked at the computer screen.

"So when would we get there?!" Mavis's frustration was growing.

"Well, I can get you on the next . . . no, the Chicago flight's delayed due to bad weather." She shook her head at the screen.

Mavis suddenly made the same crazy roaring face her dad made when he was angry.

The ticket agent didn't flinch. "So, two seats in coach?"

"No!" Mavis pulled out her poncho. She wasn't going to take three flights to get home.

"No. Yes." Johnny looked from the agent to Mavis and back again.

Mavis, wearing her poncho, quickly transformed into a bat; lifted Johnny, backpack, luggage, and all into the sky; and flew past the waiting plane.

It was a race to get to the hotel first.

The scooter rolled along, turning sharply as everyone held on.

Mavis, the bat, desperately flew with Johnny through the clouds.

The scooter hit traffic and stopped. "Come on, Blobby! Squeeze through!" Dracula instructed. The other drivers didn't even look, except for a kid in the back of a station wagon.

Mavis and Johnny flew through a rain cloud and came out the other side sopping wet. Bits of cloud stuck to Johnny's head. "Wooo! I still have some cloud on me! Gotta do a selfie—"

"Johnny! Not now!" Mavis told him as she struggled to carry him and fly at the same time.

"Okay, maybe later," Johnny agreed.

Traffic cleared, but the Blob needed to stop for a minute. He mumbled to Dracula.

"Now? When we finally have no traffic? You're killing me, Blobby!" Dracula complained.

The Blob argued.

Dracula waited, annoyed, as the Blob peed into some bushes.

Mavis heroically dodged lightning as the weather worsened. Johnny was loving every minute of the journey.

Dracula was on the scooter looking at his watch. "We're never gonna make it! Frank, blow!"

Frankenstein grabbed the Blob and blew him up like a balloon, bigger and bigger as everyone took turns climbing onto his belly.

"Now!" Dracula said as the Blob filled completely.

Frankenstein held the Blob's mouth shut and jumped on, finally letting go. As the air came out of his mouth, the Blob flew at superspeed. The monsters all hung on tightly.

Dracula was holding Dennis with one hand as they soared down the road. With his free hand, Dracula held on to the Blob, helping him steer.

The scooter took a detour through a valley. The monsters hollered with glee. They flew alongside a train, racing it as it headed toward a tunnel. The kid who they had passed in the car earlier stared at them again through the window.

Wayne mooned him.

They beat the train and got through the tunnel first.

"How fun is this?" Dracula said happily.

Filled with joy, Dracula started to tickle Dennis. Dennis laughed harder and harder.

"Why are you laughing? You like that? Watch this!" Dracula tickled the Blob, who started to laugh, which made them all fly uncontrollably through the air. The gang struggled to hold on.

Murray rolled backward and fell off the Blob. Frank

grabbed some of the Mummy's wrapping and used it catch Murray, flying him like a kite. Murray looked superskinny and extra creepy with his gauze peeled back. Dennis laughed.

"Now this is flying, Denisovich," Dracula said.

"Like a vampire?" Dennis asked.

"Like a superhero." Dracula picked Dennis up over his head. Dennis held his arms out like a superhero.

"Whee!" Dennis screamed into the wind.

"That's my boy! That's how you fly," Dracula said.

Dennis was unbelievably happy as they soared above the trees and a lake and among the birds.

It was sunset when Mavis and Johnny finally saw the hotel in the distance. Mavis frantically scanned the area for Dennis.

As the air went out of the Blob, he started flying wildly, like a deflating balloon, but somehow he managed to find a place to land at the hotel. They hit the ground hard and rolled, then popped up perfectly all together.

Dracula grabbed his phone to video chat Mavis. He saw her face on the phone. She was angry.

"So, hey, when are you gonna get here already? We've been waiting—"

He looked up to find Mavis standing in front of him. She and Johnny were at the hotel entrance.

"Give me my son," Mavis demanded.

"We just went out for some avocados," Dracula said casually.

"Mommy! I flew!" Dennis was excited.

"I saw!" Furious, Mavis held up her smartphone and played a YouTube clip titled "Dracula Remix," with more than two million hits. The clip intercut Dennis falling from a tower with rapid edits of Dracula arguing with Dana. The video had a rocking rhythmic soundtrack.

"The mother's already nutsy cuckoo," Dracula said in the video. "Nutsy cuckoo. Nutsynutsynutsy cuckoo."

As the music continued, Dracula was growing more and more embarrassed. The Blob, totally oblivious, danced to the beat as the video continued.

"That-ain't-happening. The mother's nutsynutsy

cuckoo." The video kept repeating itself.

Busted, Dracula handed Dennis over to Mavis.

"Please don't leave," he told her. He was desperate to keep her in Transylvania.

"I was worried Dennis wasn't safe around other monsters." Mavis was so mad her cheeks were red. "Now I don't even feel like he's safe around you. We'll have his birthday party here on Wednesday. Then we're moving."

Dracula looked down. He'd lost. They were leaving.

Frankenstein came over. "It's time to see Vlad."

Dracula sighed. Frank was right.

CHAPTER TWELVE

Dracula grimly drove the hearse. Frankenstein was his only friend who came along on this mission. They went down a dark, windy road that went lower and lower into a ravine. The road hit a dead end. They got out of the car and then walked down a dark hill. At the bottom of the hill they walked down a steep staircase made of stone.

The stairs ended at a large hole. They had to crawl through the hole, sliding on their rear ends, shooing away the mice and moles who nipped at them. The tunnel lead to another hole. When they came out on the other side, they stepped out onto a steep cliff.

"Oh, gimme a break already!" Dracula moaned.

They slid down the steep cliff, catching branches to slow their fall, until finally landing hard. After that, they started to walk.

"Pretty sure it's straight ahea—"

They fell through a trapdoor and kept on falling as if through a seemingly endless vacuum. Frank screamed until they hit the bottom.

In front of them was the dank cave of Dracula's father, Vlad.

"Can't believe I'm doing this," Dracula complained to Frankenstein.

Suddenly an evil-looking guard leaped out from the cave, causing Frankenstein to jump back.

"Who goest there?" the guard asked.

"It's Count Dracula," Dracula said.

"Oh. . . . Well, it's about time," the guard replied.

"Just tell him I'm here," Dracula said.

The sentry let them pass.

Dracula and Frankenstein navigated through the cave's long, spider-filled hallways. At the end of the hall, two glowing eyes blinked out in the darkness.

"Holy rabies, look what the bat dragged in!" Vlad

exclaimed, swooping forward into a shaft of light.

"Yes, hi, Dad," Dracula said without emotion.

"Fellas, you won't believe it!" Vlad said to his furry spider friends and demonic cronies. "It's the world-famous Count Dracula! Just as handsome as the day he deserted me!"

The ancient demonic monsters hovering in the shadows howled and screamed with laughter.

"Still slouching, though," Vlad said critically.

Dracula stood up a little straighter. "I'm not slouching."

"Well, this is certainly unexpected, boy. It's only been, what, six hundred years or so. Who you've been hanging out with . . . this thing?!" Vlad asked, pointing at Frank.

A couple of cronies started sniffing around Frank, making him very uneasy.

"Uh, nice to meet you," Frank said, stepping away.

"This is a monster!" Dracula said. "Frankenstein."

Vlad levitated Frankenstein high off the ground. Frankenstein screamed as the cronies aggressively volleyed him back and forth with their minds, like a beach ball.

"That's what you call a monster?" Vlad frowned. "Screaming like a frightened chipmunk?"

"Please make them stop, Dad," Dracula said as nicely as he could manage.

"All right, boys, let's not overdo it," Vlad told the cronies. "Fellas. Fellas! Come on, enough! Bela, let it go already!" Bela was clearly the demonic leader. Turning to Dracula, Vlad shrugged. "Demons. What are you gonna do?"

Bela dropped Frankenstein, who slammed down, making a crack in the cave floor.

"I'm not paying for that," Vlad said, examining the crater. "So what do you need from me?"

"It's my grandson, Denisovich," Dracula explained.

"Oh, you have a grandson! So your daughter got married? Never got an invitation." Vlad was insulted.

"Well, you know. They wanted a small wedding, and, uh, I can't stand being around you."

"All right, so what about this Denisovich?" Vlad asked, putting aside hard feelings.

"He . . . hasn't got his fangs yet," Dracula explained.

"No fangs?!" Bela mocked.

"A late fanger, Bela, it happens." To Dracula, Vlad asked, "So why are you worried? He's a full vampire, isn't he?"

"What? Uh, yes, of course." Dracula couldn't admit to his father that Johnny was human.

"So he's got till he's five. Which is . . . ?"

"Uh . . . two days. Give or take an hour," Dracula admitted.

"Two days?!" Bela exclaimed.

"Bela! I'm trying to talk with my son! Now, please— be a good dummy and play with Jiangshi!" Vlad pointed, and Bela sulked away to join another demon who was awkwardly playing a hopping game.

"Look, we're in a time crunch," Dracula said. "I need to help this along. Even if it means your way . . ."

"You mean, scaring the fangs out of him?" Vlad asked.

Dracula nodded sadly.

"Okay, what's the big deal? That's what we did for you," Vlad said.

"All right, Dad—" Dracula was embarrassed.

"Wait, Drac was a late fanger?!" Frankenstein was surprised by the news.

"Are you kidding? The latest! What, he's pretending he was always Mister Tough Guy? The boy was in love with a baby raccoon! All he ever did was hug that thing!"

Everyone laughed at Vlad's story, except Dracula, who regretted ever coming to the cave.

"Finally I had to scare the sweetness out of him. Sort of like a wussy exorcism," Vlad went on.

"Really? What did you do?" Frankenstein asked.

Dracula remembered when he was five. *He was sleeping in his kiddie coffin with a cute little baby raccoon. Suddenly the raccoon started to float out of the bunk. Dracula's eyes slowly opened to find his sweet little friend floating above him. The raccoon reached out to Dracula, when suddenly his head began to spin around. As the head spun around its neck, the raccoon turned evil and started growling and speaking in tongues. Dracula shivered in fear.*

A hand suddenly grabbed the raccoon around the throat. It was Vlad.

He brought the raccoon to his gaping mouth and started to bite down . . .

Dracula began screaming so loudly that his fangs burst out of his mouth.

Dracula shook off the memory in time to hear his father tell Frank, "I ate his raccoon. Still resents me for it."

Dracula was still upset. "Lulu!"

"Hey! You're a vampire now, aren't you?!" Vlad was satisfied with the way he'd solved Dracula's fang problem. "So, now we'll do it for the kid. Of course, I'll need his whole family present. You, Mavis, the kid's father."

"The father?" Dracula hesitated. "Eh, yes, yes, fine."

"What's the father's bloodline, by the way?" Vlad asked.

"Oh. Uh, he's a direct descendent of the, uh, Jonafangs . . . of Bucharest." Dracula was terrible at making things up under pressure.

"The Jonafangs . . ." Vlad hadn't heard that name.

Dracula quickly asked, "Yeah . . . so how about tomorrow?"

"All right, let's see . . . tomorrow . . ." Vlad considered the date, when Bela started screaming, frightening Frankenstein again.

Vlad turned to him. "I know, Bela! Tomorrow, no can

109

do. I'm booked, stealing souls all night with the boys."

Bela jumped excitedly and grabbed Jiangshi by the collar, bouncing him hard against floor and tearing his clothes off in the process. Jiangshi bounced up, naked except for his underwear, and flew off.

"Bela! Sheesh. Talk about possessed," Vlad said.

Frankenstein laughed.

"Heh. See? The fat one liked it." Vlad chuckled.

"Okay, so we'll do this on the kid's birthday," Dracula suggested.

"Fine. So give me the address," Vlad agreed.

"Okay . . . he's gonna be at my hotel," Dracula said.

"Hotel. You run a hotel?" Vlad didn't know.

"Yeah. For monsters. Only," Dracula lied. Things with his dad were so difficult.

"Well, of course, for monsters, what else would it be for? Humans?" Vlad snorted.

Vlad and all the demonic cronies laughed insanely. Dracula and Frankenstein laughed along nervously.

"Humans. . . . That's . . . a good one," Dracula muttered under his breath.

CHAPTER THIRTEEN

Mavis was packing up her old room, looking depressed. She found the dolls that Dracula had been playing with when she was in Wacky Wacky.

Dennis entered the room. "Mommy?"

She quickly pulled herself together. "Oh, hey, Dennis! I was just . . ."

"Are we really leaving after my party, Mommy?" Dennis asked.

"Yes." Mavis tried to sound cheery. "But do you know who's coming to the party? Daddy's whole family! Grampa Mike and Grandma Linda, and all your cousins and uncles who love you so much. And then they're gonna be with us when we move to California!"

"Okay . . . but what about Papa Drac?" Dennis asked.

"Papa Drac will visit us," Mavis told him. "And we'll visit him. Why don't you go get ready for bed?"

"Bed? I didn't have dinner yet," Dennis complained.

"Oh . . . right." Mavis frowned. It was going to be a long night.

A suit of armor entered, holding a bowl.

"Madame. Your father realized you hadn't eaten all day, and so he made you this." The suit of armor handed her the bowl of monster ball soup. Mavis took it and started to cry. The monster balls started to cry as well.

Mavis and Johnny stood in the dining room, welcoming Johnny's family to a nice dinner. It was the night before Dennis's big birthday party.

Johnny's family all sat at a couple of long tables pushed together. Dracula was walking around, greeting everyone. Mavis was uncomfortable but acting cheerful. The Phantom of the Opera played the pipe organ. He sang with great passion.

"The night brings Johnny's family here
To take away all that Drac holds dear
Hide your feelings, keep them all inside."

As the adults had adult conversation, Dennis sat next to his cousins Troy, Connor, and Parker.

"Dude, why do you wanna leave?" Troy asked Dennis. "This place is out of control!"

"I don't wanna leave!" Dennis wailed.

"All these awesome freakazoids!" Parker exclaimed, looking around the adult table.

"So who's the coolest monster?!" Connor asked.

"Kakie!" Dennis shouted with joy.

The others laughed hard. Dennis immediately realized he should've thought before blurting that out.

"Kakie! What a wuss-bag!" his cousins said.

Dennis didn't want to talk to his cousins anymore. But his dad was busy talking to Grampa Mike.

"We'll have to find a progressive school out there," Johnny said. "We're raising Dennis with the Educare method, so we never say no, but we never say yes. We only say 'no-es.'"

"Mmm-hmm. Sounds idiotic," Grampa Mike replied.

Dracula interrupted the conversation. "Hey, guys! I just need to borrow Johnny for one minute."

"Just one?" Johnny asked, disappointed.

Dracula zipped Johnny away quickly to talk privately.

"Okay, I spoke to my dad," Dracula whispered, looking around to make sure no one was around.

"What? You have a dad? That's funny." Johnny laughed.

"Yeah. He's a riot. We have a plan." Dracula was serious.

"Yay! Awesome! What do we do?" Johnny wanted desperately to stay in Transylvania.

"Terrify the boy until we scare the vampire out of him." That was the plan.

". . . herrihy huh hoy . . . ?" Johnny stumbled over the words.

"Yes. And by tomorrow night, he'll be a full vampire," Dracula said confidently.

"Drac, that sounds harsh, man . . ." Johnny wasn't so sure he liked the plan.

"Do you want to wear shoes?!" Dracula nearly shouted the question.

Johnny took a deep breath and looked at his sneakers. "I'm doing this for you guys."

"Okay. So . . . terrify . . . what does Dennis love the most? Besides us." Dracula needed the information to tell his father. "And. No. Raccoons."

Johnny looked around the room. "Okay. Well . . . there's Kakie. We booked him for the party."

"Perfect. Oh, one more thing . . . ," Dracula started.

"What's that?" Johnny asked.

"My dad cannot know you're a human," Dracula said with half a smile. "Or any of your family."

"What? But Drac, I'm proud that we—"

Dracula interrupted Johnny. "Or he'll eat you. All of you. I'm not kidding."

Johnny rushed back to his family's table. "Guess what, gang, Drac and I just decided we're gonna make the birthday a monster masquerade party!"

"Really?" Mavis asked.

"Oh, that's lovely. Sort of like a last hurrah before Dennis gets to be with normal people!" Linda loved the idea.

Dracula mumbled, "I couldn't have said it better."

Mavis looked ashamed. Dennis was totally bummed. The Phantom of the Opera continued his song.

"Smile through the pain
Your daughter feels the same
But neither will dare to say it . . ."

Dracula gave him a look to change the song, but the Phantom didn't notice.

CHAPTER FOURTEEN

It was Dennis's birthday!

The hotel guests, monsters and humans, were all dressed as monsters. They were enjoying the party along with Johnny's family. Mavis wanted to fit in with the humans, but it was so awkward. They were wandering around the ballroom, acting like zombies. It was weird. Then, suddenly they all broke into silly laughs.

"What do you think, Mavis? I'm starting to like being creepy!" Linda chuckled.

Mavis smiled and nodded. It was just too much.

Across the room Dennis, dressed as a Batman-y superhero, was not getting much attention. While the other kids played together, Dennis was playing Batman all by himself.

"You're lucky we don't call the authorities!" he said in a voice like his Papa Drac. "Let's go, my hero!" He went back into his own voice. "Cebause I'm Batman!" Then, as Dracula again, answered himself, "Yes! To the Batmobile!"

Suddenly Winnie knocked Dennis over and licked his face. The cousins laughed. Mavis looked at Dennis sympathetically.

Troy, dressed like Vrak, a freaky TV show villain, snickered. "Got your butt kicked by a girl, Batman!"

Winnie *grrrr*ed like a dog at Troy.

Troy was freaked out. He hurried away, saying, "Yeah, uh, whatever. I'm not about to cry."

On the road to the hotel, Vlad and Bela, the demonic crony, stopped to look at the hotel from a distance. Bela was carrying Vlad's "medical" bag.

"So . . . this is the hotel my son is running? What a waste." Vlad shook his head, distressed.

"Tear it down!" Bela suggested.

"Oh, Bela, you want to tear down everything." Vlad sighed. "Let's just get this over with. And on the way out, grab some towels."

Back in the ballroom Dracula was talking to Johnny, who was dressed like a very strange-looking vampire.

"So, what do you think?" Johnny asked.

"This is your vampire costume? What are you, nuts?" Dracula looked him over.

"I ordered it online! It was the only place that delivered overnight," Johnny explained.

"You look like you got a baboon's butt on your head!" Dracula wrinkled his nose. "Have you at least practiced your voice? You can't just talk like a hippie."

"I'm not a hippie," Johnny said. "I'm a slacker."

"Talk like a vampire!" Dracula insisted.

Johnny tried it. "My name is Count Jonafang! I am a vampire!"

"Okay, vampires don't go around saying, 'I am a vampire!'"

"Sorry," Johnny apologized. He tried again. "I am Count Jonafang! Bleh, bleh-bleh!"

Dracula rolled his eyes. "Are you kidding me?"

Johnny apologized again. "I'm sorry! I'm nervous!"

"Yeah, listen, if you think *I* don't like it, you definitely don't want to say 'Bleh, bleh-bleh' in front of my father," Dracula warned.

The suit of armor announced, "Sir, Master Kakie has arrived." The suit presented the guy who played Kakie on TV. He was a dull-looking man with a big costume bag. He looked bored and tired.

"Oh, hey. Drac," Johnny introduced the Kakie actor, "this is Brandon, a.k.a. Kakie."

"Hey, man," Kakie greeted.

"Kakie, uh, Brandon, this is the man himself, Count Dracula."

"Right on. Cool." Kakie was in a hurry. "All right, so when does this happen? I got a book fair in half an hour."

The doors to the ballroom suddenly burst open, revealing Vlad, wind whipping his cape. Bela was trailing behind. The room was immediately quiet.

"All right, are we ready to do this?" Vlad asked in an announcer voice.

Dracula saw his father come in. He sighed. "Always has to make a dramatic entrance." He shouted across the room. "Oh, yeah, wait right there. I just gotta do one thing." He quickly asked Frank, "Keep him away from . . . avis-May, and the . . . umans-hay."

Frankenstein replied, "Ot it-gay. I'll . . . ake sure he doesn't know they're humans in disguise-may."

"Okay, your pig latin needs work," Dracula told Frank.

"Yeah, I failed it in high school," Frankenstein said. "Sorry."

Before Dracula could get across the room, Mike and Linda reached Vlad. "Oh! Now that is a neat costume."

Frank pushed his way between Vlad and Johnny's parents.

"Hey, Count, how goes it?" Frank jogged Vlad's memory, just in case. "Frankenstein. Remember me, from the suffering . . . ?"

"Ah. The floor-cracker," Vlad remembered.

Frankenstein took Vlad to meet his friends.

"So, lemme introduce you to some of your son's other buddies." Frank stepped aside. "This is Murray . . ."

Murray shook in his gauze. He acted cool, but it sounded crazy. "Hey, V! Excuse me. Heard that hole you live in is off the chain, dawg."

"Talking toilet paper—well, that's a new one." He pushed past Murray. "All right, where's the kid? Where's the family?"

"Johnny!" Frank called him over. Murray was afraid of Vlad, but Johnny was even more afraid. "This is Dracula's son-in-law . . ."

"Johnny?!" Vlad didn't understand the unusual name.

"I . . . am Count Jonafang! Bleh blehhh—blacksheep. Have you any . . . wool?" Johnny did his best accent.

"What's on your head?!" Vlad laughed.

Everyone also laughed, but they didn't get the joke. They were all scared.

"Not funny. Your generation is sick." Vlad walked over to the stage and started setting up his fang ritual.

Dracula was helping the Kakie actor get into his costume.

"Okay, we're ready to go, just one thing," Dracula said.

"Sure, let's make it quick." Kakie wanted to get out of there.

"Okay. You just have to stand in this one spot. The whole time." Dracula showed him a mark on the floor.

Vlad finished setting up thirteen red candles. He mumbled to himself as he sprinkled some items around the candles. "Mugwort . . . ancient earth . . . elk blood . . . monkey nuts . . ."

"Okay, one spot? Dude. Kakie's all about using the whole space," the actor said.

"I know, but it's the acoustics," Dracula said. "They can't hear you unless you're right here. See? Now . . ."

He moved off the spot and pretended to talk in a loud voice, to show how there was no sound. Dracula mouthed, *"You can't hear me."* He stepped back. *"But now you hear me perfectly."*

Kakie gave in. "Okay, dude. But none of these parents better review this on Yelp."

Dracula said, "Johnny, start the show. Kakie's ready."

"Kakie? But the big kids, they're gonna—" Dennis said.

Johnny interrupted. "It's all good, it's all good. Kids, everyone, have a seat. Dennis has a big surprise for you.

The one and only—Kakie the Cake Monster!"

Some younger kids cheered loudly as Kakie entered and stepped onto the place Dracula had shown him. The older kids were not amused.

"Hey, kids! It's me, Kakie! What a wonderful Kakie day it is!" Kakie wobbled on the spot.

Winnie smiled encouragingly.

"Now, I have a question. Who here loves cake?" Kakie asked.

Only a couple of kids got excited. And the Blob. He was excited too.

"Meeee!" shouted the kids.

The Blob shouted blobbish gibberish.

"Rise!" Vlad suddenly made Kakie float up above the kids and toward the candles.

"Whoa, whoa! Why am I floating?" Kakie looked down, slightly panicked.

Suddenly Vlad made the candle flames burn more brightly. The flames formed a circle around Kakie.

Kakie grew more panicked. "Whoa, why the flames? Can I have the stage manager please? This isn't working for me!"

"Yes! Awesome! Burn Kakie!" the cousins shouted.

"Crowd's loving it, Kakie! You got 'em right where you want them!" Dracula clapped for the show.

Vlad made the flames higher, scaring Kakie. Kakie called down to Vlad, "Dude, are you doing that? It's freaking me out, man!"

Vlad swept his arms in front of the candles. "Behold! Remove the poisonous spirit of Kakie from this fangless child!"

"Scary, huh, Denisovich? You feeling anything? Any change?" Dracula stared at Dennis's mouth.

"Is Kakie okay?" Dennis worried.

Johnny and Dracula looked at each other.

"Johnny, who is that guy?" Mavis got close to her husband.

"Oh, it's just your dad's, uh, dad," Johnny said casually.

"What?! I have a grandfather?" Mavis stared at Vlad.

Vlad pointed at Dennis and said, "Bring forth the monster from within!"

Kakie's costumed head began to spin. Even the cousins gasped. Dracula looked concerned.

"Aaaaugghhh! Dude, stop spinning my head and

you can just pay half!" Kakie wanted to go home. Immediately.

With a wave from Vlad, suddenly the cake guy morphed into something evil and really, really scary.

He was possessed. "I want all the cake! Sharing is for the weak and cowardly!"

That did it. Dennis jumped into Dracula's arms.

"I'm scared, Papa! What's happening to Kakie?!" Dennis asked, burrowing his head into Dracula's shoulder.

The show wasn't over. Vlad hopped onto the stage and grabbed Kakie. He opened his mouth wide.

He was about to bite off Kakie's head!

Kakie screamed in horror. "This guy's gonna eat me!"

Dennis closed his eyes tightly.

Dracula was stunned for a second, but then he leaped forward. "Stop it!" he shouted at his father.

Dracula put out the flames with a hand wave.

Everyone stared for a long moment.

"'Kay, I'm leaving! This was bogus!" Realizing he was still levitating, Kakie Guy started "swimming" out of the room.

"What did you just do? I was gonna eat the guy's head like we talked about! And the kid's fangs would pop out!" Vlad stared at Dracula.

"I don't care! It's not worth it!" Dracula told his father.

"What's not worth it?" Mavis came over to Dracula and Vlad.

"It was my last attempt to make the boy a vampire so you'd stay," Dracula admitted.

"By scaring him into it?! How could you do that?" Mavis was furious.

"It was the only way," Vlad told her.

"Stay out of this," Dracula told him.

"We were desperate!" Johnny said.

Mavis was shocked. "You were in on this?"

"Dennis won't be happy in my town!" Johnny turned to her.

"Dennis hasn't been there!" Mavis countered.

Just then the Phantom of the Opera started singing.

"Now husband and wife
Feel the strain and the strife—"

"Shut up!" Johnny, Mavis, and Dracula shouted at the same time.

"Johnny, Dennis is not a monster!" Mavis stomped her foot.

"He'd rather be here!" Johnny said.

"He likes avocado!" Mavis said, stomping her foot again.

As they argued, Dennis scooted away from them all.

"'Cause you don't let him eat anything fun!" Johnny told Mavis.

Grandma Linda cut in. "Johnny, I think Dennis just wants to be normal!"

Grampa Mike told her, "Don't say that! He is normal!"

"Can we stop using the word 'normal'?" Mavis argued.

"Where we live now, he's normal!" Johnny told her.

Quietly Dennis left the ballroom. No one noticed except Winnie. She went after him, and together they ran away.

"He is who he is! And you can't change him, Dad!" Mavis was still arguing with Dracula.

"But I don't want to lose him!" Dracula told her.

"It's not always about you, Dad!" She was very upset.

CHAPTER FIFTEEN

Outside the hotel Dennis ran away as fast as he could. He wasn't going in any particular direction, just deep into the woods.

Winnie yelled at him as she hurried to catch up. "Dennis! Where are you going?"

He was crying. "Away!"

"Dennis, you'll get killed out here!" Winnie shouted at him. "Come on! Follow me!"

Winnie moved ahead of him, leading the way to the dog fort.

At the hotel Vlad said to Dracula, "What about the shame that boy brings you?"

"There's no shame. I love him no matter what. And he loves me. And I'm not going to mess that up," Dracula answered.

"Love? This is not about love. It's about tradition," Vlad said.

"No! That's where you're wrong. It's about family. Something that you drove away," Dracula retorted.

"You call this a family? It's a bunch of rejects." Vlad snorted at his son.

"They're my rejects!" Dracula looked around the room. "When the world rejected monsters, I protected them here while you hid in your cave. They're all my family now. Monsters and humans."

Vlad sniffed toward Linda. "Humans? That's what that horrible smell is!"

"Hey, back off my mom, old man!" Johnny bravely got in Vlad's face.

"Johnny, be cool." Dracula tried to keep things calm, but Johnny tossed off his wig in anger and challenged Vlad.

"You wanna throw down? Certified yellow belt since 1997!" Johnny struck a pose.

"No!" Dracula stepped in to stop the fight.

Vlad looked at Johnny, now without the vampire costume. "What's this, now? You're not a vampire either?"

"Uh . . . Bleh?" Johnny tried the accent.

"Of course he's human, he's our son." Grampa Mike was now in the fight. "You think we're monsters?"

Grampa Mike and Grandma Linda dumped their outfits.

Vlad started screaming at Dracula. He was so, so, so mad. "You! You've ruined our bloodline! Thousands of years, tossed in the trash!"

Vlad's face made a big vampire roar, like Dracula sometimes did, but unlike Drac's face, Vlad's was really scary. "This place! You've let in humans, who torch us and hate us—"

"They don't hate us now, Dad!" Dracula tried to explain.

"You're a fool! This hotel should never have existed!" Vlad was screaming so loud his voice echoed through the hotel.

"Destroy the hotel!" Bela shrieked.

His voice summoned the other demonic cronies. They laughed as they came to the castle.

Everyone was terrified.

"These guys are insane. I know exactly what to do," Frank said. "Hide." Frankenstein dove under a couch, which was half his size.

The demonic cronies flew toward the hotel.

The building started to shake and rumble as the cronies got closer and closer. A few pieces of the building crumbled off, nearly hitting some scared party guests.

When they reached the hotel, the cronies burst in, smashing through all the ballroom windows. Everyone started screaming. The Blob, frightened, ran off, leaving a pile of Bloblike poop where he had stood.

Dracula looked at Vlad. He was more angry than ever before.

"Witness! Humans coexisting with monsters! Sharing towels and spoons!" Vlad showed the cronies around the room.

The cronies screamed in anger and disbelief.

"Johnny, grab Dennis! Dennis?" Mavis looked

around. Where was he? "He's gone!" Mavis cried.

"Dennis, buddy, where'd you go?" Johnny scanned the room.

Dennis sat at a little table in the dog fort. Winnie poured tea for them both.

"It's much quieter away from all those people," Winnie said. "Why do they wanna take you away?"

"Cebause my mommy said I'll be happier in California," Dennis told her.

"You're happy here! With me!" Winnie leaped up and knocked him down.

"I know. But I think they think, they think I'm not happy, cebause I don't have hair on my face like you. I'm sorry. It's my fault." Dennis rolled out from under her. He looked at Winnie sadly.

"No! You are perfect! You're the nicest boy I know. And I have three hundred brothers." Winnie sat down across from him.

"You're nice, Winnie," Dennis said.

"We should just hide here together." She showed

him a stash of dog food cans in the corner. "Forever. I packed snacks to sustain us here for years."

"Okay. Maybe, Winnie." Dennis considered it.

"It's all zing," Winnie said with a smile.

In the ballroom the cronies were ransacking the party, destroying the hotel, punching holes in the walls, ripping columns out of the ground. Suits of armor, witches on brooms, and zombies rode flying tables in a battle to stop them.

But the cronies were out of control.

The Human Fly buzzed around, annoying a crony.

Murray blasted sand at some cronies. The sand pushes them back briefly, but they kept coming back. Griffin stood behind Murray, swinging a candlestick.

"How do we stop these guys?" Murray asked the others. "Nothing's working."

Griffin said, "We have to keep fighting!"

"Dad! You can destroy this place, but you'll never break what we built here!" Dracula roared.

"You are such a fool," Vlad told his son.

"No. You're a fool," Dracula said. "Because you won't change, and because of that you lost me and the chance to know your granddaughter and your great-grandson."

Meanwhile, Mavis and Johnny were frantically looking for Dennis.

"Dennis! Buddy? Dennis?!" They took turns calling his name.

"Dad, we need to find Dennis!" Mavis cried.

Dracula's eyes went wide. "What?! Denisovich is missing?!"

Dennis stood by the window in the dog fort, looking outside. Winnie brought him a tray. "I made you dead pigeon for dessert."

She showed him a plastic dead pigeon on a plate.

But Dennis wasn't interested. He was staring out the window toward the castle. He squinted and looked hard. There was smoke and dust.

"What's the matter, Dennis?" Winnie asked.

"I think something bad's happening," Dennis told Winnie. "I think we need to go back."

"If you think so, my zing. I'm right behind you!" Winnie followed Dennis out of the fort, and the two of them hurried back toward the castle.

Dracula was a human. The cronies were running wild. The hotel was in shambles.

Eunice was hitting a crony with her handbag. "FRAAAAAAAAANNNNKKK!" she shouted for her husband.

Some of the cronies held their ears in pain, but they continued ransacking.

Mavis, Johnny, and Dracula were running around, avoiding cronies and looking for Dennis at the same time.

"Denisovich!"

"Dennis!"

Wanda suddenly realized something else. "Winnie?"

Just then Dennis and Winnie entered the hotel.

Mavis saw them from across the lobby.

"Dennis! Baby!" Mavis and Johnny shouted at the same time.

Dracula, Mavis, and Johnny all ran to hug Dennis as

Winnie ran to her parents and gave them a hug.

"You're okay!" Dracula held him tight.

"Papa! What's happening to the hotel?" Dennis saw the mess.

"Don't worry about the hotel! I'll build a new one," Dracula told him. "I'm just happy you're okay."

"Even if I'm not a vampire?" Dennis asked. He looked deeply into his grandpa's eyes for the answer.

"I don't care if you're a vampire," Dracula said. "You're my grandson. My perfect, beautiful grandson."

It seemed like it would all be okay, until suddenly Bela swooped down, grabbing Dennis.

Winnie tried to help Dennis by biting Bela's hand. Bela screamed and flung Winnie away, knocking her to the ground.

Dennis was upset. "You better not hurt Winnie, cebause—"

"HAHAHAHA! Cebause what?!" Bela made fun of Dennis.

"Cebause . . . ," Dennis began.

"Cebause nothing! Cebause you're a weak, little . . . human!" Bela was not letting go.

Dennis closed his eyes, summoned his anger . . . and suddenly made a fierce red-eyed vampire face like his grandfather. He growled like Dracula! And then, he bared fangs!

Suddenly exploding with power, Dennis slammed the demonic crony with his mind, sending him flipping across the room!

Everyone was shocked.

The other cronies attacked Dennis, and he defeated them one after the next, dodging them with superspeed, pounding them with superstrength, and making them freeze like ice cubes.

"Woohoo! He's a vampire! Awesome!" Johnny exclaimed.

Grampa Mike and Grandma Linda looked at him curiously.

Everyone was amazed as Dennis crushed the cronies with lightning speed. Punching, kicking, mind controlling, zapping—Dennis was everywhere and taking out all the demons.

He zapped them together into a bundle and blasted them through the roof.

Everyone cheered.

Dracula, Mavis, and Johnny took turns congratulating Dennis.

"I did it! I really am a vampire!" Dennis was so happy.

"No, my boy. You are a superhero!" Dracula told him proudly.

"You kicked butt, little man!" Johnny said.

While everyone celebrated, Dracula looked around the room. "Where's my father?"

"Over here!" Johnny hurried over to Vlad. He helped him out from under a pile of weapons and rubble.

"You? You saved me?" Vlad stared at Johnny.

"I sure did, Gramps," he said.

"And with this?" He held up Johnny's backpack. It was riddled with weaponry.

Johnny was horrified. With tears in his eyes, he grabbed the backpack.

"Nooo! Backpack! You're gonna make it, buddy. MEDIC!" He hugged his pack, cradling it like a baby.

"Dad, I'm so sorry. He is like us." Mavis looked again at Dennis's fangs. "You were right."

Dracula said to Mavis, "No, baby. We all wanted to

tell Dennis who he was, instead of letting him find out for himself."

"Did you just call me Dennis?" Dennis cut in.

"Yeah, he called you Dennis! He realizes he was wrong!" Vlad told the kid.

"Yes. Only I was wrong," Dracula moaned.

"All this pressure about when the boy's fangs were coming out. Who cares? Mine came out years ago!" Vlad pulled out his false teeth.

"Okay, Dad, please. Put 'em back in before we all barf." Dracula gagged.

Suddenly Bela emerged from some rubble. He grabbed a broken lance as a stake and flew straight toward Dracula.

In the last instant, he was zapped by Vlad and raised high up in the air.

"Don't ever come near me or my family again!" Vlad turned Bela into a ridiculous-looking miniature version of himself. The wolf pups immediately started throwing him around the way the cronies had tossed around Frank.

The humans and monsters celebrated with hugs and congratulations.

Griffin was kissed by an actual human girl. He fainted.

A huge birthday cake was wheeled in by the gargoyle chef.

"Well, we may not be leaving, but it's still Dennis's birthday! So . . . everybody . . . ," Mavis was saying, when everyone shouted, "Happy birthday!"

Suddenly the old gremlin lady grabbed the entire cake, interrupting the singing.

She licked her lips and grinned. "I didn't do that."

The party ended with singing and dancing. It was a terrific night.

Dennis was five.

He had his fangs.

And he was ready for his next adventure.